Hello everybo[...] genuinely thank you [...] Our Wake. It means the most; I can't even begin to put into words how grateful I am. Instead of writing a gushing essay about how grateful I am as an author's note, I'll keep it simple.

Thank you, from the bottom of my heart,

Aiden Kruppe

This book goes out to all of the grandmas out there. I know I wouldn't be here without the love and care of mine.

Chapter 1

Devon's sickness started mild. His symptoms quickly advanced from a dry heaving cough, to puking, to spitting blood. He now lay in his room, surrounded by doctors and shamans alike. My family is in severe debt and can't pay for the service, nor product of medical officials. So, they offer them our heirlooms, food, even to bed with them.

My name is Dylan, and I've been put into quite a precarious situation. My country, Parlania, is under siege by the evil god Scaf and his army of Resurrects. They gain ground on us daily, slaughtering any Parlanians in sight. I'm told I'll be conscripted soon, and to prepare to fight, but I cannot. I refuse to leave my family like this. Devon needs a cure, Father needs money, and Mother needs rest. If things continue this way, Devon will succumb, Father will be arrested and slain for being heavily indebted, and Mother will wither away from exhaustion. As for me, I am useless. I tend to the fire in our stove, and go shopping. Otherwise, I'm told to stay out of the way. I'm called a disgrace for not leaving to fight against the Resurrects, even by my own family. It stings, but what else am I to do? I have the choice to die fighting for Parlania, and let my family die, or stay with my family, doing nothing but collecting insults like shiny pins.

"Dylan! Water, now!", Mother's frantic yelling snaps me out of my groggy trance. I was laying in bed, going over everything that had happened recently. "Devon needs water, hurry!" I jump to my feet, and fly down the hall. Grabbing an iron pot from the counter with one hand, I shove the musty, wooden door open with another. It creaks as it shoots open, and shakes as it closes with a slam. I sprint to the well, and hastily begin raising the rusted bucket.

    Whenever Devon began to choke on his own blood, water helped clear his throat out. Because of this, Mother has to watch him at night. The pail reaches the top of the well, and I dump the water into the pot. The pot becomes slightly heavy, but that doesn't slow me. I use my foot as a hook on the bottom corner of the door to open it and speed-walk towards Devon's room. I tried not to slop water on the dirt floor, as nobody likes stepping in mud. Nearing Devon's room, his coughing became louder. Mother holds the door open for me as I enter. She then runs to Devon's bedside and holds his mouth open. This proves to be quite the challenge, as his head is constantly convulsing with his choking wheezes.

    As I pour water into Devon's mouth, he gargles, still choking. Eventually, the water forces its way to his stomach, and Devon begins to hurl. Gory puke lands all over, soaking the blankets and wooden bed frame. Devon began to inhale loudly, regaining his breath. I sat on the floor, put the pot on the ground, and wiped my sweaty forehead with my hand. Mother instantly assaults, "You couldn't have done that any faster? If your father had any money, I'd buy a slave to do this. Is that what I need to do?

Should I whip you like a slave, boy?" I solemnly responded, "No, Mother." I tried my best, why was she berating me? This happened every time she asked something of me. It was never done well enough, nor fast enough. I can't do anything right. Mother scoffed, then demanded, "Leave us, boy." I followed instructions.

After setting the pot back on the counter, I sulked back to my room. It was late, and the house was dark. Not being able to see well, I stub my toe on the corner of my doorway. I don't yell, although I exhale loudly. I lifted my foot to my stomach, as if that would heal it. Once I was finished squeezing my foot and silently seething like an idiot, I crawled into bed.

I was filthy, covered in dirt and sweat. I can't remember the last time I bathed. At first, it was hard to sleep this dirty. Now, it was normal. I had gotten to the point where I couldn't even smell myself anymore. Father told me I wasn't worth the water, and I didn't argue. Last time I incited that I disagreed with him, he slapped me as hard as he could.

I lay in bed, staring at my ceiling. When does it end? When will it finally get better? Did I do something wrong? Is this all my fault? This ran through my head rampantly, night after night. No matter the amount of contemplation, I could never answer any of these questions. It seemed as if there was no solution, and nothing more to life than to serve and suffer. Little to my knowledge, you had to take respect. Beat it from those who refuse to surrender it, and kill all who deny it. This lesson would soon be taught to me.

CHAPTER 2

I was sitting at our cruddy wooden table, stirring my stew made of rotten carrots and tiny rabbit chunks. It was disgusting, but it was food. Father sat to my right. He was a fairly strong man, with black curly hair. I'd seen him beat three men he owed money to, all at once. He was stern, and quick to resort to physical harm if me or Mother disobeyed.

Mother sat to my left, nearly falling asleep at the table. She was incredibly slim, and was visibly sleep deprived. She always insulted me, no matter what I did. She had untamed blonde hair, much like her temper. I was also fairly skinny and had blonde hair. I'm 17, which means I could get drafted into the army. I couldn't bring myself to scream at someone like Mother, nor hurt those wrongfully like Father. Perhaps that's why we are in this situation; I just can't grow up and assert myself.

Father looks at me and barks, "It's already mixed boy, just eat the shit." Mother fires back, "Shit? This is the best meal we've had in months!" If I had a golden coin for every time I heard them argue, I'd have enough money to pay off Father's debt, buy Mother a nice bed, and give Devon the attention he so desperately needs.

Father drops his spoon and gestures to the bowl in front of him, "Please woman, you couldn't cook to save your life! It's a miracle from Parla himself that you haven't poisoned me yet!" I began to eat the foul concoction, as Father would beat me if I didn't follow his orders.

Mother unsteadily stood up and shouted, "I'm trying! Maybe I could buy better ingredients if our money wasn't sitting upon every gambling table in the village!" Mother wasn't wrong, Father liked to gamble. Swiftly rising from his chair, Father threw his spoon at Mother's head. He retaliated, "My pastimes are none of your concern, bitch! I try to win us money, and I will one day!" Mother responded, "You won't win money, all you'll do is lose your head. You'll lose your cock too, if you don't sit down and eat!" Father violently flipped his bowl over, throwing stew across the table. He walked out the front door and tempted, "Eat that." He was most likely leaving to the bar to spend what little money he had on cheap booze.

Mother shriveled into a ball on the floor and began to wail. I stood up and offered comfort in the form of my hand on her shoulder, only for her to slap it away and scream, "Leave me! I don't want your pity." Doing as I was told, I left in pursuit of Father. I was positive I'd find him drunk, but maybe I could find work at the bar. Sometimes people needed their gardens weeded, and I could snatch a few vegetables, or their houses dusted, to which I could steal small valuables. I didn't like stealing, but it's the only way I could get by. It's always good to have a few coins, sometimes Father likes to take them from me. When I don't have any, he usually attacks me. I threw on my deer hide toga and thin wooden sandals, then departed for Ray's Bar.

Chapter 3

Ray's Bar was busy, per usual. The village's drunks often gathered here to swap tall tales, along with drink until they couldn't stand. I never understood alcohol. Everyone claimed it helped them quit thinking about their problems, but all drunk people do is talk about their problems. The bar was fairly well kept, and smelt terribly like cigars and inexpensive ale. I slid past people, making sure to apologize to anyone I bumped into, until I reached the knucklebones table.

As I suspected, Father was sitting in his typical spot. After placing his last dice, Father's face sank. I had never seen him so afraid, and for a reason that was unknown to me. There were two other men at the table, and they both looked at each other and smiled. One of them was weasel-like with a thin, wiry, reddish mustache. The other was slightly chubby and bald. Both were dressed like they belonged in the capital of Parlania, along with the other rich men.

The mustached man stood up and said, "You know what that means. You're 50 gold down the drain, along with the other 150 you owe us from the last two games. Now, I suggest you pay up, or we might have a problem." Father stood up, shaking the table and sending his chair to the floor behind him. Matching the tempo, the larger man stood up. I could sense the strings of tension binding the three men together, and they wouldn't let go until someone cut them.

Rather than cutting the string, Father tightened them further by saying, "Well, is there something you'd like to do about it? I'll take you both at once. If I win, the debt disappears. If I lose, I owe you double." I might not always agree with Father, but this seemed like a bet he couldn't lose. The bald man teased, "You can't pay double, punk" Father smiled and coaxed, "I won't need to, I can handle two girls at a time, Chubby." I might not be the brightest, but I know innuendo when I hear it.

Father and the two men walked outside and behind the bar. After evading people and trailing them, I peeked around the corner into the alley. Father was kicking the scrawny man on the ground, and the larger man was standing back. Chubby whistled loudly, and laughed. Armed men came out of the shadows, from behind trash bins and out from windows.

Chubby claimed, "You're a damn good fighter, but you can't take 12 of us. Now, how about you give me 150 gold instead of the agreed upon 200, and I'll turn you loose." Father spit on the ground. What was he doing? He couldn't beat 12 men! Suddenly, someone tapped my shoulder. I turned around to be met with a priestess holding a grail of a reddish liquid. She whispered, "Parla wishes to speak with you."

I was bamboozled. Why would Parla, my God, want to speak to me? Where did this woman come from? Why now? What was even happening? Confused or not, it was disrespectful to decline the will of a God, so I nodded, not sure of what was happening.

    The robed priestess extended the grail towards me, showing me my reflection in what I knew to be blood. Parla was the God of Blood and Wrath, after all. The second I saw my reflection, I knew something was wrong.

    Instantly I found myself in a barren landscape. There was nothing to be seen in any direction, other than a sea of knee-high red grass. A figure rose from the painted grass, as if it was being birthed from it. The man wore no clothes, other than a red cape and a red cloth around his midsection. The man was muscular, and wore a serious expression. It was Parla!

    I dropped to one knee and threw my gaze to the ground. Parla commanded, "Up, son. I have a question for you." I slowly stood up, and made sure not to insult Parla with my stare. Parla continued in a deep, echoing voice, "Aren't you sick of being the pawn?", he circled me, "Aren't you tired of being demoralized? Hit?" I stood in silence. I could feel the blood rushing to my face in embarrassment of being speechless. Parla stopped. He eerily laughed and said, "I thought so. The equation is at your feet. The answer runs in their veins. Use it wisely, son. I'll be expecting you."

    As if no time had passed, I was once again staring into the grail of blood. The priestess retracted the grail and stated, "I'll meet you later. May Parla protect you." The odd girl ran off. Everything happened too fast for me to understand. I just talked to my God, rather than listening to him talk, and he spoke in riddles.

I felt something weigh down on my toes. Looking down, I saw a sword. It had an odd separation in the middle, almost as if a sword had been cut in half, spread half an inch apart, and been attached to a hilt. I carefully picked up the blade. It was heavy, and extremely sharp. Remembering what Parla had said, he told me that "the equation is at your feet." Did he mean this sword?

Father inhaled in pain after being hit. Wasting no time, I lifted the sword and walked into the alley. I had never held a sword before, but I think I was doing it right. I yelled at the men surrounding my Father, "Hey! Get away from him!" They all looked at me, then laughed. One of the men drew a blade of his own, followed by another. Soon, every man had some sort of armament. Their lengths and widths all varied, but their purpose was shared; to harm.

I was about to drop the sword and run, but my blood began to pump quickly. I could feel my heart beat speeding, thumping inside my chest. I walked forward, no, something forced me to walk forward. Two of the men matched my approach, and held their edges up. I didn't know how to fight! A small voice whispered, "Just let me guide you. You've nothing to lose, do you? I reckon that is what makes you so dangerous." It sounded oddly like Parla. Listening to the voice, I continued to walk.

The first man charged, lifting his sword over his head, ready to split my skull in half. I used my sword to block the attack, and then kicked the man in the chest. The blade didn't feel as heavy as before. The man fell to the ground and grunted.

The next crook grabbed and threw a knife from his belt, to which I deflected with my steel "equation". What was I doing? The voice whispered, "The answer to that lies in their veins". The man slowly approached me, holding his sword with two hands. He swung first, straight across the horizon. I rotated my wrist to the left so that the sword faced downwards at my side, blocking the attack. I then cut upward, hacking the man's sword arm clean off. He screamed in agony, grasping at his stump. This scared me, but I didn't stop. I thrust the sword forward, straight through his throat. The gap left room for his windpipe, so I was allowed to hear his howls for a few moments longer, until he collapsed.

I heard the man that I kicked get back on his feet and lunge from behind. I stepped to the side, and the man shoved his sword into the wall. I then swept upwards across his elbows holding the sword. His hands impressively still limply held the sword, although they no longer held onto his body.

Before he could react, I pulled his sword out of the wall, and shoved it in between his ribs. Blood poured out onto my hand. The feeling of warm blood invigorated me, almost as if it saturated my every need. I unsheathed the commoner's weapon from his chest, and threw it like a dart at another man sprinting towards me.

It stuck into his knee. He toppled over, landing at my feet, and looked up. He stuttered, "W-why are you doing this?" The answer lies in his veins. Not liking mystery, I thrust my sword into his face. Blood climbed the blade, and wove around my hand. I felt further empowered. With the attackers attention diverted, Father stood up. I expected him to help, but instead, he ran the other way. I just saved him, how could he?

Infuriated, I walked toward the remaining bandits. Three of them ran the opposite direction, which was a smart move. That left six more. Six more beings with blood jailed inside of them. I intended to liberate it.

I started with the mustached man from the bar. He held a small, thin blade that matched his physic. Backed up to the wall, dropping his blade, he lifted his hands and begged, "Please, there's no need. I-I've got money, see?", dumping his pockets onto the ground. I commanded, "Pick it up." He got onto his knees and scrounged the gold. He lifted it in both hands above his head. I took the gold, and put it in my pocket.

When he went to stand, I pressed my sandal against his face, pinning it to the wall. Two men charged at me, thinking I was distracted. In one sideways slash, I turned them into half the men they used to be. Their organs piled at my feet, and their blood climbed my legs. The man against the wall scaredly questioned, "What are you?" The answer lies in his veins. I took my sandal away from his head, only to stomp it back, bashing his head into the wall. The man yelled, "Okay, no questions! Please, let me leave!" He began to sob. I stomped again. His head smashed open against the wall, sending an artistic splotch of blood in each direction. The man tried to crawl and escape, but I stomped again. This time, his skull wasn't so durable. Blood and brain matter painted the wall, finishing my masterpiece.

Three remained. Three more times I could feel this bloodlusting high obtained from slaughter. I wonder, if I inflicted grizzly wounds, would the effect be greater? The leftover men were clearly afraid. Chubby ran the opposite direction rather slowly. He could use the exercise.

I let my sword down at my side, and stood still. The men stared at me, and I stared back. I ordered, "Kneel." One listened instantly, and the other argued, "Are you crazy! Look what happens when you kneel!", and pointed to the headless body. This bothered me none. Instinctually, I cast my sword forward. A stream of blood fired from the split in my sword, creating a spiraling laser. It pierced the man's stomach first. It then exited his back, and reentered, only to emerge again from his torso. The bloody vine continued to turn the defier into a pin cushion. With each impalement, the man jerked. I swiped my blade to the right, and the blood contracted, cutting the man into little bits.

His blood fed the dirt alleyway, morphing its pigmentation. The other man remained on his knee. I had no reason to kill him, he was already afraid of me. I turned the other way, and began to walk home as if nothing happened. As I left, the mystical sword sucked into my wrist, and what felt like directly into my bloodstream. I could feel its presence flow through me, almost as if it was passing through my veins. Could this be the answer to all of my problems?

Chapter 4

The sun was tucked in underneath the horizon like a blanket, peeking out slightly. It cast an orange which transmogrified into a pink across the sky. It was a brisk night; the chilly wind kept nipping at my skin. Our house was at the end of the dirt paved street, and wasn't anything special. It was one floor, made of thin oak, and pretty small. Its placement was nice though, as the well was close. The forest behind us blocked the Western wind.

During the winter we all huddle around the fireplace, trying to stay warm. It seems that the only time my family can get close, is when we are freezing to the point our toes are numb. I opened the door, and entered. Father was sitting at the table next to Mother. They both looked at me with very different gazes. Father was fearful, Mother was skeptical.

Mother began, "Alright, why did your Father pull me from Devon's bedside so that I could see you?" I stood idle. How could I explain that Parla talked to me directly, gave me some sort of sword, and a vile bloodlust? Father kindly demanded, "Show her, boy." Father had never talked to me with an ounce of respect in his voice. It made me feel good.

Instinctually, I throw my hand downwards, and the sword leaks out of an opening in my wrist, forming in my hand. Once it was finished, my wrist closed again. Mothers face went white. Father couldn't take his eyes off of my red steel. After being afraid of my parents for so long, I enjoyed being feared.

Mother asked, "H-How? What witch did this to you?" I responded plainly, "Parla." Mother gasped and held her heart. Father shook his head and shamed, "You made a deal with a God? Praise Parla, but you know that's a terrible idea." I countered, "There was no deal, Parla asked for nothing in return other than to see him again tomorrow. I think he wants me to go to the palace in town square." Mother warned, "You shouldn't, it's surely a trick" My parents have never seemed to care about me so much. Father argued, "Nonsense, do as Parla wishes. Disobeying a God is a great way to get us killed." I called the sword back to its sheath.

Father shook his head, "To think our measly son was blessed by Parla." I fired, "Measly? I saved your ass!" Father slammed the table and yelled, "Language! I will take no such disrespect!" Mother asked, "What do you mean, Dylan?" I didn't owe her an answer. Instead, I continued, "What are you going to do about it, Father?"

Father stood up and approached me. He raised his hand as if to hit me. I put my left hand up to block the incoming assault, and my left wrist opened. Instead of a sword, a circular shield appeared in my hand. Father punched the shield, then retracted his hand in pain. Mother bolted to Devon's room and locked the door. She knew when Father was angry, she'd end up getting beaten too.

Father yelled, "Put that shit away!" I lowered the shield to my side, but taunted, "I could kill you with the flick of my wrist, choose your next action wisely." Father looked past me at the floor. The smell of smoke infiltrated my nose.

I looked back to see fire crawling up the door. Father chanted, "Fire! Fire! Get out of the house!" Mother yelled from across the house, "I've fallen for that trick before, I won't leave this room!" Father dove through the kitchen window, and into Mother's flower pots. I heard them shatter as he landed on them. The fire engulfed the kitchen quickly, smoke blinding me. I dropped to my knees and crawled toward Devon's room.

I pounded on the door, and Mother gasped. She began to wail, "Please, not again! I did nothing wrong!" I continued to pound on the door, until a chunk of wood broke loose. Reaching through the hole, I unlocked the door. I opened it and crawled into the room. Smoke crept on the ceiling behind me.

Mother stated, "Y-You weren't lying!" I grab Devon from his bed, to which he begins coughing. Blood lands on my toga, which makes me quiver. I didn't want Devon to bleed, but it felt so good. I set him down outside of his window, and motioned for Mother to go next. Mother climbed through the window, and I followed. We ran to the front of the house to where Father was.

Chubby was standing with two other men, all holding torches. He threatened, "See what happens when you owe?" I yet again took my sword out, accompanied by my new shield. Chubby yelled, "It's him again! You can't hide behind that freak forever! When I find you alone, I'll kill you myself!" I continued to walk towards them. The arsonists all turned tail and ran.

Chapter 5

Black smoke ascended from the burning cottage, illuminating the clear, starry night. The moon sat behind the house, peeking at me through the smog. My hands dropped to my side as I watched the roof cave in. Mother was also entranced by the scene, but Father was enraged.

He yelled, "Dylan you little shit! You shouldn't have let them go!" I turned around and flatly stated, "You could've stopped them, but you ran." Father looked down in defeat. Mother asked, "Where are we to go? We can't sleep outside."

A familiar figure tapped me on the shoulder, startling me. It was the priestess again, donning her white silk robes. Her face was wrapped with a silk mask, only allowing her eyes to show. She whispered, "Parla wishes for you to stay in his palace." Father strided toward the priestess and asked, "Us too, right?"

The priestess shook her head in denial. "No, just Sir Dylan. I'm sorry, but it's Parla's wishes." Mother joined Fathers side with Devon in her arms. She begged, "Please, Dylan, take us with! We won't cause any disturbance, I swear!" I looked at the ground and debated.

Mother and Father only started being nice to me when I had something to offer. Why should I take them with me? They're only my family. They hit and insult me, why would I ever help them? I looked Mother in her blue eyes and defied, "No."

Mother scoffed, "You'd leave us here to die?" Father raised his hand to hit me, but retracted it when I lifted mine. The priestess beckoned, "We really should get going, Parla is eager to speak with you." I nodded farewell to my family, and turned to walk with the priestess.

Mother yelled as I departed, "You coward! You look out for no one but yourself! You can leave, but you better not come back, boy!" This didn't bother me, as I looked for every opportunity to escape her. I guess an encounter with the God of Blood was the push I needed.

As we neared Parla's palace, the surrounding buildings began to gain tiers, and their architecture advanced. The paved dirt road turned to cobblestone, which turned to stone bricks. The palace came into sight as we took a corner. It was made of marvelous marble, and stood at least triple the height of the buildings surrounding it. There was a grand staircase that led to its large entrance, littered with people praying and leaving offerings to Parla. Other priests and priestesses were talking with commonfolk, most likely offering advice and counsel. I had only been to Parla's palace once before. I was here with Mother, begging for someone to cure Devon. It was embarrassing.

I climbed the stairs behind the priestess. She motioned for me to enter and whispered, "This is as far as I go, Sir Dylan. May Parla protect." I nodded in gratitude, and continued up the stairs. I entered the palace through two massive birch doors. The main room had a marbled floor, with a red rug leading to a throne. On it sat Parla.

This time it was really him, not some blood-construed apparition. He wore a brilliant white toga, decorated with golden pins. Guards armed with spears and tall shields lined the rug. I'm sure they were there for looks, rather than functionality.

Parla beckoned in a deep voice, "Come, son. I've been waiting." I trotted towards Parla and asked, "Why couldn't my family come?" Parla answered plainly, "I despise people like your Mother and Father. I'd sooner have intercourse with a cheese grater than house them." That was a fair point.

Parla continued, "Besides, it's you I want to see. I offer a simple trade, one that benefits us both." Father warned me of making deals with Gods, but he wasn't here now. I neared Parla's throne and asked, "What is it?" Parla had a blob of curly black hair on his head, and a beard to match it. Scars littered his body, presumably from battle. He had golden eyes, as all Gods do. Parla sat forward, and held his own hands.

"My offer is simple," Parla said, "Lead my men against Scaf. Use this power I've given you to repel the Resurrects, and I'll cure your brother's ailment." I shook my head in disbelief and asked, "But why me? You could've picked anyone." Parla answered, "Because I know you're the right one for the job. You have nothing to lose, and everything to gain. All you have to do is give me a blood offering." Parla whistled. A priest entered the room holding a small dagger and a bowl. He offered it to me. Parla asked, "Well?"

I nervously giggled and said, "Is there any way I could sleep on it? Seems like a rash decision, right?" Parla's face sank in boredom. He sat up straight, and folded his arms. "So be it, take him to a room." Parla commanded.

The priest gestured to a hallway with his hand and led, "This way, Sir Dylan" I have no idea how the priests knew my name, but I wasn't about to start asking questions now. All I was worried about was rest.

I was given a room with a bright red carpet, along with a large bed. A window showed the stairway, which was still populated. A dresser made of polished birch wood sat across from the bed, and atop it was a platter of finger food. Grapes, crackers, and even small meat slices. Enticed by the food, I grabbed the entire platter. I sat on the grandiose bed, and began to munch away.

Chapter 6

I woke up with my hand resting on the empty platter. I felt bloated, but full. I haven't felt full in my entire life, it was a new experience. For once, maybe I ate too much.

I sat up, stretching my arms above my head, then straight in front of me. I felt great, the bed was the most comfortable thing I'd ever slept on. I got up, put my sandals back on, and set the platter back on the dresser. A knock at the door stole my attention. I opened the door to be greeted by a priest, different from the one from last night. He whispered, "Parla asks that you wash and dress today, if you would follow me to the baths, Sir Dylan." I eagerly nodded my head.

The priest led me down long hallways decorated with statues and paintings of Parla and his accomplishments. One painting in particular had all of the Gods, the dysfunctional family that they were. It showed Seebes, Goddess of Bounty, Ruler of Tilithia, next to Scaf, God of Death and leader of the Resurrects. Behind them was Parla, the eldest brother. Behind him was Helena, Goddess of Creation. She ruled over life and nature, and lived high on the lightning-infested clouds. The father of the family was Modus, God of Nothing. Modus hides in his burrows deep inside the Crystal Caverns. His face was a black splotch on the artwork, as if no one should see him. The family fought more than my own. It is said that the family used to be bigger, but they killed each other off for their land, then wiped their names from history.

The priest opened a door for me, and steam flooded out. He whispered, "Enjoy, Sir Dylan. Clothes are sitting on the bench when you are finished." I thanked the priest, and hurried into the room.

There was a large inground bath made of marble and outlined with gold. Hot water streamed from a small group of holes in the ceiling. There were small alcoves toward the top of the pool that kept it from overflowing. The dense air was slightly hard to breathe, but that was a price I was willing to pay to finally feel cleansed.

I dipped my toe in the hot water, then stepped down into it. The toasty aqua felt superb on my feet. I took my toga off and descended down the pool's stairway into deeper water. I allowed the pool to swallow me up to my neck. I washed myself, but made sure to do it slowly. I wasn't going to waste what could be the only hot bath I'll ever have.

A bar of soap that smelt of pine trees sat on the edge of the pool, which I used to scrub myself clean. There was an odd liquid next to the bar of soap, but I wasn't sure what it was for, so I left it. I wet my hair. As the bathwater ran down my face, I realized this is the most peace I'd ever been given. I was alone, clean, in a gorgeous palace, with nobody to tell me what to do. I had dreamed of being a wealthy man with my own house before, but never did I think it would be this great!

I wrapped myself in a towel, allowing the steamy air to dry me the rest of the way. The room was humid, but in a good way. Not too dry, nor too moist. I wonder how much a bathroom like this costs? After drying and enjoying the controlled climate, I dressed in the toga left for me on the bench. It was extremely comfortable, presumably made of silk. I couldn't say for sure, as I had never worn silk before. A silver pin held the toga closed. Pleasantly polished sandals were also set on the bench, much nicer than my personal pair. Rawhide straps held them on my feet, rather than scratchy twine. I bid the room a sad farewell. It genuinely took effort to leave.

The priest sat outside the door in a chair, twiddling his thumbs. He stood up as I exited, and quietly complimented, "You look exquisite, Sir Dylan." I silently thanked the priest by smiling and nodding my head. It was awkward that strangers were saying kind things to me, although I did like it.

The priest led me back out to the throne room. It seemed as if Parla hadn't moved from his throne all night. As I approached, he waved everyone away. The armed guards marched out of the room in a uniform line. Parla waited until everyone had abandoned the area to talk. He asked, "So?" The truth was, I hadn't thought about it much last night. I was too busy enjoying food and the luxury of comfort.

After everything Parla had done for me, I could do something for him. Parla offered my brother health in return for a soldier, and he got it. I shook my head, "Yes."

Parla snickered and said, "Good. But I require one thing from you first, think of it as a test. I want you to find the fool who burned your home, and I want you to kill him. That'll prove to me you have the ability to seek vengeance, along with not being afraid to kill. Life is only as valuable as you perceive it to be. Consider it worthless, and it's easier to take."

I knew that was a disgusting way to view life and murder, but Parla wasn't wrong. He was a God, could he be wrong? "I accept.", I boldly stated. Parla's eyes widened, and a smile grew on his face. He radiated the feeling of amusement. A priest approached me holding the same dagger and bowl as yesterday, and offered it to me.

"All I need is a blood offering. Consider it collateral." I took the dagger, and the priest held the bowl with two hands above his head and he got on both knees. I went to cut my palm open with Parla interjected, "Ah, wait. The wrist, boy. I take it you don't mind?"

I moved the blade to my wrist, and slowly slid it across. This made me wince. Blood began to seep out of the opening, and dribbled into the glass bowl. After Parla motioned his hand to the priest, the priest gave me a bandage to cover my wrist. I handed the ritualistic dagger back to the priest, and wrapped my wound.

The priest walked up to Parla, and gave him the bowl. Parla sipped from the bowl until it was empty. I thought it was weird that a God was drinking my blood, but I guess today is full of new experiences. Parla handed the glassware back to the priest.

Parla said, "So it's settled. Kill your father's attacker, and return to me. Do not come back empty handed." The last part was said in a threatening manner, which slightly scared me. Parla watched me stand idle, and prodded, "Well? Go!" I obeyed, and left the throne room, down the staircase.

Next time I visited Parla, I'd have killed more people for wanting what they were owed. I was doing the world a favor by removing violent gamblers, right?

CHAPTER 7

I started in the alleyway where I first encountered Chubby. Royal guards littered the area and were questioning patrons. Luckily, it was hard to get a straight answer from a belligerent drunk. I figured I might not want to take a direct approach, considering royal guards were everywhere.

Standing across the dusty road, I observed the scene for a way to get close without getting caught. There was no way to get to the alley on the ground, which left the roof. I couldn't reach the roof from the ground without climbing something, but the only thing around Ray's Bar were more buildings. I walked up and down the opposite street scouting for a way to the rooftops. At the very end of the street, there was a hovel with an arch-supported roof. Connected was a little storage shed, which was about 6 feet tall. I cross the street with a slow jog, making sure not to draw attention to myself.

I jumped up and grabbed the board that served as a roof for the outbuilding. I tried to lift myself up, but failed. Dropping down, I shook my hands and hyped myself up. I jumped again, falling almost immediately. On the way down, I got a nasty sliver. I pushed and pulled the toothpick-sized stabber out of my palm. I thought it was deep enough to make me bleed, but I didn't. I looked to see if anyone was looking.

First things first, I must wait for the royal guards to clear out. While I waited for this to happen, I crept back towards the top of the roof. I layed on the side that faced the forest that eventually led to Tilithia. I continued to watch the sky, and slowly, accidentally, drifted to sleep.

Chapter 8

Rain began to dribble on my face. I woke up to gray clouds, which looked much less inviting than the open sky. Slowly, the rain started to fall faster. I stood up carefully, making sure not to slip off of the roof.

Looking down, I stared at where the glimmering object was previously. It was no longer shining, as it was partially submerged in mud. I lowered myself from the building using my hands above a dumpster. I dropped onto the dumpster's lid, and then down to the drowning ground.

As my sandals made contact with a puddle, dirty water flew, painting my new, lavish toga. This slightly irked me, but I didn't dwell on it. I walked to the trash can I was gawking at earlier, and picked up the item next to it. It was a silver military patch with the name SAMSON engraved. It was a gorgeous medal. Unfortunately, someone misplaced it. I held the patch tight, and returned to Parla's Palace.

Upon entering, Parla was still seated in his throne. He beamed as I entered, "Well? Any progress?" I explained, "I found a medal from one of my Father's attacks-" Parla cut me off, "You are doing this for you, not your Father." I assured, "Yes, I know. Anyways, I plan on asking some people around town if they knew who it was. I'll act as if I just want to return it to avoid suspicion. After getting a name, I'll get an address. I'll then ask where Chubby is." Parla interjected again, "And when he remains loyal to this Chubby you speak of?" I replied, "I'll get my answer, I assure you that." Parla smirked and concluded, "Good. You appear to be sopping wet. I'll have a priest come to your room with fresh clothing. I trust you remember the way to your room?" I nodded. Parla waved me away, and I took off for my gifted resting spot.

I made sure not to sit on my bed, as I didn't want to drench it. Instead, I stood patiently, watching out the window. No one was outside, which made perfect sense. The rain was rather cold, which leads to sickness. Puddles formed in the street, washing away travelers' footprints. It was now pouring from the dense, dark clouds. Occasionally, thunder would clap and echo throughout the entire village. Sometimes it would surprise me, making me flinch.

A knock came at my door. I opened it, and an unfamiliar priestess handed me a set of clothes, identical to my current set. All that was lacking was freezing dampness. She also gave me a towel, which I appreciated. I thanked the priestess. She nodded, and left. I closed the door as she departed.

After undressing, I used the towel to dry myself off. I threw my new garments on, and sat on the edge of my bed. I stared at the name on the medal: SAMSON. Whoever Samson was, I hoped for his sake that he was feeling cooperative. I wanted, no, needed answers. If finding Chubby meant curing Devin, I had to do it.

Chapter 9

Once I woke up, I repeated yesterday morning's routine. Bathed, ate some grapes left for me in my room, and left for Ray's Bar.

The storm had passed, but it was still awfully muddy outside. The damp air felt nice in my lungs. For some reason, breathing after a downpour always felt pleasant. I made sure to walk towards the sides of the road, avoiding any puddles.

Once I reached the bar, I began to get cold sweats. I was never in a bar when Father wasn't there. It was odd that my drunken Father offered subconscious comfort to me. I entered the bar, putting on a facade of confidence. I started at the poker table, looking for any familiar faces. I wasn't so fortunate. Studying people, I made my way past tables surrounded by middle-aged men talking in slurs.

Eventually I approached the bar table. Father never really sat up here, he said these seats were reserved for snide asshats. I never had any proof of this, but I took his word for it.

I took a seat next to an older man. His hair was grayed and thinning, and his breath smelt of mead. He had lost some of his beverage on his shirt, but didn't seem to care. I wasted no time, boldly questioning, "I found this outside, and want to return it to the rightful owner.", showing him the medal.

The man paid me no mind. He tapped the table with his knuckles and said, "Two more. One for me, and one for the kid with a death wish." The bartender did what was asked of her. I accepted the kind offer and asked, "Death wish?" The elderly man warned, "That Samson boy runs around with some of the gamblers. He ties up loose ends in the form of killing those who owe. Think of him as a sort of mercenary, just paid in nasty women and alcohol." I disregarded the warning and furthered my interrogation, "Where can I find him? I'd just like to return this." The man took a sip of his drink, notioning I should do the same.

I slipped the drink towards him and repeated, "Where can I find him?" The man set his mug down, looked me in the face for the first time in our conversation and claimed, "You don't want to find him. Most of the time, he'll find you first. I know what you did, and trust me, he'll get you first. You don't want to find him, you want to find his boss. I might be old, but I'm not stupid."

I stood up abruptly, attempting to startle the man. He paid me no mind. Insulted, I knocked his empty mug off of the bar table. I beamed at him. "Walk to the end of the left end of the road. Three houses down. I didn't tell you that." I patted him on the back, to which he grabbed my arm and demanded, "You didn't hear anything from me." I pulled my arm from him, and left.

I didn't notice until now, but almost everyone had been watching us. I wouldn't tell this Samson punk who told me his location, but I'm sure other patrons would.

Part of me felt bad for the old man. I reminded myself that if he had told me what I wanted to know, I wouldn't have had to make a scene. Surely he did it to himself, right?

Chapter 10

Wasting no time, I followed the old man's directions. I walked around wet patches of dirt until I reached the end of the road. The road curved to the left, which I followed.

People littered the streets, taking care of daily tasks. I passed a mother carrying groceries. She nodded to me, and I returned the favor. I counted three houses, and knocked on the door. It was a smaller abode, not much larger than my family's. I knocked again, louder this time.

The man with blonde, wavy hair answered. He didn't open the door all the way, protecting himself. He asked in a tired voice, "What?" I held up the medal and asked, "Recognise this?"

He went to slam the door in my face, but I stopped it with my hand. I threw the door open, and the man slowly backed up. He grabbed a knife out of his knife block to defend himself.

I slowly walked towards him and said, "Samson, I presume?" Samson nodded. A female voice yelled from a different room, "Who is that?" Samson yelled, "Go back to bed, whore!" There was no response. I stopped a few steps away from Samson. I said calmly, "There's no reason for that. You know what I want to know. Tell me, I give your medal back, we both walk away." Samson grabbed a second knife from the block, hinting he didn't want to talk. Whether his blood or his information first, what he spilt that was up to him.

    Samson threw a knife at me, and it stuck in my right shoulder. He took another knife, and darted it into my left shoulder. Blood didn't escape my holes. I pulled both knives out, and threw them to the ground. They clattered on the floor. Blood didn't coat either weapon.

    Samson stuttered, "W-What are you?" He held two more knives high to defend himself. I answered, "Someone who's going to hurt you real, real bad."

    I swiped my hand at Samson's head as my sword appeared. Samson ducked, and drove a knife into my side. I used my free hand to pull the blade out, and stuck it in the table. Samson backed away. I stabbed forward, but Samson evaded to the right. He shoved his last knife into my elbow. This time, his attack proved trouble.

    The blade locked my elbow in place. My sword was stuck straight out infront of me. I formed my shield, and slammed it horizontally into Samson's throat. He clutched the table for support, along with his neck. I drove my shield down onto his back, knocking him to his stomach.

    "Would you like to talk now?", I prodded. The light voice yelled once again, "Now what the hell's going on?" Samson slammed the table and demanded breathlessly, "Shut it, wench!" I used my faulty arm to chop Samsons fingertips on the table off. He instantly went upright and yelled in pain. Blood ran down his hand and pooled on the floor.

I stepped closer to Samson, pinning him against the wall. His blood climbed my legs, and pushed the blade out from my elbow. I retracted my weapons, and grabbed Samson's hair. I beat the back of his head off of the wall. He grunted in pain.

Footsteps came closer, into the kitchen. A woman's voice screamed, and then footsteps ran away. Instinctually, I picked up the blade wedged in the table, and threw it. It landed in the girl's back, dropping her. I then put both hands on Samson's throat, and lifted him off of the ground.

"I'll try again.", I asked seriously, "Where is he?" Samson choked out, "Fuck y-yourself-f." I dropped Samson back on the floor, and monotony stated, "No." I socked him in the gut twice, to which he bent forward. I pulled his face into my knee. His head bounced off, and I lifted him by the neck once again. Blood streamed from Samson's nose, and onto my hands. I demanded, "Answer me." Samson tried to swing at me, but I was just out of reach.

I lifted him higher with one hand. His feet dangled, kicking wildly. I used my newly free hand to punch his stomach repeatedly, as hard as I could. He winced each time, but couldn't draw in any air. I dropped Samson, to which he fell to his knees.

Samson gasped for breath, but I kicked it out of him. I yelled this time, "Do you want to lose your entire hand?" Samson didn't respond. I drew my weapons again, but a fingerless hand was held up to stop me.

He wheezed, "Big house at the end of the street, real nearby. Just leave me alone." I replied, "Wasn't that hard, was it?" I turned to walk away. Samson stood up slowly behind me, and dashed for me. I turned and intercepted him with my sword. My weapon entered in between his ribs, and exited his back. Blood leaked from his wound, along with his mouth. I retracted my sword back inside me, causing Samson to drop at my feet. Blood pooled on the floor for me to absorb. It seemed the only way to get the answers I wanted was to kill. It didn't scare me, which scared me.

Chapter 11

I returned to Parla's palace. I figured I had made decent progress today, which earned me some rest. This time, Parla wasn't seated in his throne. This was abnormal. I made my way to my room. My toga had holes in it, along with wet splotches graciously donated from Samson.

The sun was just starting to set outside my window. My platter had been filled again, this time with smoked ham and corn. I feasted on my bed once more, gushing over the amazing flavor. Each bite was like a nugget of gold in my mouth.

As I went for another chomp, a rapping hit my door. I set my food down on my dresser and answered it. It was the same priestess from the other day.

"Parla said you might like a new outfit, Sir Dylan.", the priestess said, offering me a new set of clothes. I took them, and turned away. The priestess asked, "Parla was wondering if you'd made any progress." I turned and said, "I'll talk to him tomorrow." I shut the door. I'm not sure the priestess deserved that disrespect, but I'm not sure I cared. They were nothing but slaves anyways. I always thought Parla's worshippers had high prestige, but they were nothing more than servants. I didn't realize this until now.

I changed out of my crimson plastered toga and put the new one on. The feeling of silk was beginning to lose its initial novelty. I wonder if there is a better, more comfortable material? I slid my sandals off, and plopped down on the bed. I got comfortable, only to realize I forgot to grab my dinner plate. I sat and contemplated if I wanted the food that badly. The ham was amazing, but I'm extremely content. Soon, I sucked it up, got back out of bed, grabbed the food, and returned to the bed. I sunk back into the soft mattress, almost as if I had never left. What was I so worried about?

    After finishing my supper, I gently tossed the platter like a frisbee at the dresser, landing it on the top. I burped obnoxiously and covered myself with the thick, red bed sheets. All I could think of was my family. Where were they? No one in their right mind would let them stay at their house, not with Devon's sickness. It was also unlikely that Mother and Father had any actual friends that would let them stay at their dwelling anyways.

    It was toasty and cozy under the blankets; much nicer than the chilly, damp weather outside. After a very physical day and some hot, gourmet food, I was ready for some much deserved rest. Not before long, I fell asleep.

Chapter 12

I stood before Parla seated in his throne. I had taken care of my typical morning routine, and intended to inform him of my progress. He looked down on me from his throne, wearing his usual smirk.

"I found the owner of the medal. He led me to Chubby, although he didn't want to. I'm going to his residence today to confront him.", I relayed. Parla corrected me, "To kill him, confront isn't the right word."

It felt as if all Parla wanted was blood, regardless of who it was. He was dangerous, no doubt about that. I nodded, and turned to leave, but Parla interrupted my departure, "Ah, one more thing." I turned back to him. "You've earned this.", Parla stuck his hand out at me, almost as if he was casting some sort of spell. I felt my temperature rise, heating my core. I could feel my arteries pumping harder than usual. Parla retracted his hand, and motioned with it to leave.

I turned back, wondering what Parla had done to me. I'm sure I'll find out soon. I set out to return to Samson's house, then follow his directions.

The roads had dried up by now, covered in flaky mud. People were walking the entire street again, rather than avoiding puddles. Occasionally, someone would look at me with shifty eyes. I didn't pay them much mind. Soon they wouldn't dare to look at me, not without repentance.

I found myself passing Samson's house, and walked directly past. Nobody had found the bodies yet, which was good. That made it so that I wouldn't have to hide. Following Samson's instruction, I went to the end of the street. No one else walked down this far.

Chubby's house was large, and made of stone bricks. It was obvious that he was rich. Two men stood at his door in loose togas. They were both tan, muscular, and bald. They watched me as I approached the door. I attempted to walk past them, but they both put their hands on my shoulder to stop me. I allowed them to push me back into the street, but I didn't lose my balance. I neared again, and the guards put their hands inside of their toga's. They were threatening to reveal a weapon. This didn't scare me. I continued to walk. If they moved against me, I'd kill them.

They both drew shortswords with hilts of silver from their clothes. My wrists opened, and my weapons appeared. Nothing seemed new. They swiped in unison, to which I blocked with my shield. They must've trained to fight as a single unit, which was commendable. One sliced from right to left, the other opposing.

I stepped backwards, and they stopped the attack, avoiding cutting each other. I raised my sword and shield, waiting for another. If I attacked first, one would defend and the other would retaliate. As I predicted, they lunged forward, swords first. I used my shield to redirect one of the attacks, and my sword for the other. Before they could recover, I kicked the rightmost goon. He hit the ground and exhaled as the air was knocked out of him. I wasted no time, throat punching the left-side guard in with my shield. His open hand went to grasp his neck, but I shoved my sword into his torso. Blood traveled up my sword, directly into my bloodstream.

      I backed off and let the remaining guard stand. He grabbed the fallen one's sword. He now dual wielded sharp edges. This time, he awaited my attack. I set my sword on top of my shield and advanced slowly. I swung from over my head and down. The guard crossed his swords, and intercepted the blow. He slid his blades up mine, forcing it back up. He then went to shove his blade into my stomach, but something quickly stopped him. A tentacle, much like the one from the alley, formed at the front of my shield. It wrapped around the blade and yanked it, tossing it to the side. This had almost seemed unfair, but I wasn't going to complain.

      The guard backed up to the door. For some reason, he didn't seem afraid. By now, the sparsely populated streets had completely emptied. I assumed the commoners saw danger and fled. I held my shield out again, commanding it to kill the guard. Nothing happened. I tried again, to no avail. I shook it off and sprinted towards my enemy. He deflected my first attack, and my second. I stabbed him in the throat, but the guard ducked. He then shoved his sword into my stomach again, only for my shield to save me in the same way. His sword thumped as it hit the dirt. Unarmed, I cut the guard's head off. That too, made a thump. Blood climbed my leg, and went into my wrists with my weapons. It seemed the tentacles only worked when I would be killed. But then again, I was able to command them earlier with ease. I'll have to ask Parla later.

I kicked the headless body to the side so that I could get into the door. I opened the door to be greeted by a disturbing sight. It was a large dining room that was much nicer than my own. At the table sat Chubby, joined by my family. Guards stood behind my family with small daggers at their throats. Chubby sat at the far end of the table with his hands on the table. I didn't dare to move fast, otherwise my family might be killed. I sat down at the opposing end of the table, and stared at Chubby, awaiting his dialog.

Chapter 13

Chubby began, "I'm a businessman. Let's talk business, shall we?" I disliked his tone, but there was nothing I could do about it yet. I asked, "Where is Devon?" Chubby assured, "He's resting in one of my rooms. He doesn't need any more problems. Funnily enough, he could be the only one who survives this."

I knew better than to trust this swine, but I had no other option. Chubby took a cigar out from his jacket and lit it. After taking a sizable drag, he continued, "Now, you've killed a handful of my employees. A lesser man would have already slit their throats.", he motioned at my parents. He continued, "I want one simple thing. Give me double what your Father owes me, and we all walk away. You work for a God now, surely you have the money." Father spoke, "Please do it." I stated, "I owe you nothing, Father. Why don't I just let them kill you?" Mother budged in, "It wouldn't be unlike you, you ungrateful shit!" I had nothing to thank them for, so her words were empty air. Chubby asked, "Well?" I said, "Done,"

I stood up to walk over to Chubby, but he stopped me, "No, slide it across the table. One movement and I'm dead, I'm smarter than that." In all reality, I didn't have any money on me. I also didn't know how much my Father owed to double it.

I sat back down. I admitted, "Good thing you're smart, that was what I was going to do." Chubby took another puff, flicked his ashes in an ashtray, and said, "Yes, I know. I also know you care not for your family. I just wanted to try and get what I was owed, but that clearly won't happen. Kill the woman." I slammed the table and shouted, "Do it and I'll kill you all!" My Mother's keeper looked to Chubby for instruction. Chubby shook his head.

    He continued, "So then what do you offer me? There has to be something." I said, "What if I set royal guards outside your home, surely you have plenty of people that want to kill you." Chubby laughed, "I already own them, I don't need that. How about one of those priestesses? I'd love a night with one." "They aren't under my command.", I told him. That was the truth. "You're wasting my time.", Chubby insulted, "You have nothing I want. I'm done here." Chubby stood up and pointed at both guards, and ran into a hallway, out of sight. The guards drug their daggers across the windpipes of my parents.

Chapter 14

Blood swept its way down their throats and onto the floor as I quickly donned my weapons. My parents were absorbed into me. I threw my sword at my father's assailer. It plunged into his head. In a fit of rage, tentacles shot out of my free hand, returning my sword to me. I launched myself at the other killer, and slid my sword down his torso and stomach. I used my sword and shield as a wedge to pry him open. He screamed in agony as I tore his heart out. Their blood fused with mine. For some reason, I wasn't upset with my parents death. I was almost relieved.

I began to pursue Chubby down the hallway, but another guard came around the corner. I thrusted my sword into his jugular, absorbing his blood. I continued down the hallway into the kitchen. Two more men stood there. They grabbed lengthy kitchen knives.

Tentacles shot out from my sword's gap, and grasped them before they could attack. I squeezed them until blood poured from their noses. I continued up a staircase.

I was met by another hallway with three doors, all closed. I kicked open the first one. An empty bathroom. I kicked open the next. It was a grand bedroom, also empty. I kicked the final door in.

Chubby sat next to my brother's bed. I could tell he wasn't going to do harm to him. Chubby calmly stated,

"You know that I knew you'd make it here. You passed the test, you can go home now." "What the hell are you talking about?", I asked. Parla suddenly appeared behind me. I asked again, "What is this?" Parla explained, "I paid Chubby here to do this. I had chosen you from birth to lead my armies, I just had to wait until you were ready. Now, prove it to me."

    Chubby stood up and yelled, "Hey! You said I wouldn't actually die!" Parla recited, "I'm a businessman. Kill him, Dylan " Chubby took out a small knife, and held it above Devon. "I want my life, you want the boy. Let's make a trade. We are businessmen, right?" I snagged the knife with a tentacle. "Turns out I'm a better one.", I said as I shoved my blade into Chubby's forehead. Chubby crossed his eyes as he looked at my sword. I recalled my armaments.

    I turned to Parla and yelled, "What the hell was that?" Parla retorted, "Watch your tone boy. Your brother is safe, those who held you back are dead." I attacked, "You mean my parents are dead!" Parla nodded and repeated, "Watch your tone, boy. I'll prove to be much harder to fight than these mortals. Now, Devon will be taken to my palace and given help. I'll keep him alive until you win my war. After that, I'll heal him. You have my word." I yelled, "Your word clearly means nothing! Look where your word got him!", I motioned to the carcass on the floor.

PAGE 52

Parla lost his smile, and stepped towards me. He threatened, "You will kill for me, and that's that." "If I don't?", I challenged.

Tentacles like my own sprouted from Parla's back, and wrapped around my neck. Little needles entered my throat, and my blood ran cold. Parla answered, "Or I'll kill you, and find another. You are nothing but a piece on a chessboard to me. Not a pawn, but maybe a horse. Hell, you could even be a rook if you'd like. You forget that I am king." I went to use my sword to slice my binds, but I couldn't. My veins refused to open, almost as if they were poisoned. The tentacle needles reversed the action, now sucking whatever toxin they injected me with. I could feel my heart beating again. Parla let me go, and angrily left the room.

It seemed that I was just a servant to Parla, just as his priests and priestesses. I wasn't in control of my own life like I believed. All of a sudden, I realized that I wasn't in charge of as much power as I believed.

Chapter 15

I carried Devon out of the house, taking care to not allow him to see Mother and Father's bodies. I began walking back to the palace. By now the sun was setting behind the trees. Sometimes Devon would cough up some blood. Suddenly, it all made sense.

Parla said he had chosen me. He knew my parents were terrible people, and would beat me. That would motivate me to seek help. Parla then used his powers to make my brother bleed internally, which was his leverage. He'd keep him alive as long as I obeyed his command. I've experienced nothing but an awful life, all because Parla needed a general to fight his war for him, and there wasn't a thing I could do about it. Once again, I felt helpless.

As I climbed the staircase to the palace, I realized I didn't want to be here any longer. I was a captive, no different than a slave. The worst part was, if I had just listened to Father, I wouldn't be here. So would he.

I walked into the same sight I always did: Parla seated in his grandiose throne, surrounded by guards. A smirk sat upon his face. Now that I knew of his cunning, I had an urge to wipe it off. Parla waved towards Devon and I. Priests came and grabbed Devon from my arms. I attempted to follow them as they took him to a room, but two heavily armed men stopped me.

Parla said, "Down to business. Scaf's forces rally less than a day outside of Parlania. I'm told there are around 12,000 men, not including calvary and siege machines. The royal guards, my guards, and militia come to only about 9,000 strong. You'll join General Starfli to help her whip the troops into order." The word "her" hung around in my head for a while. I haven't heard of a female general, well, ever. This intrigued and worried me at the same time. Parla continued, "Together, I expect you to halt the Resurrects. Once that is done, we can plan on how to push them backwards." I nodded.

I had heard of the Resurrects and how fierce they were. Their souls never died, only their corporeal being. Scaf collected souls of the dead who he saw fit to serve in his army. He blessed, or cursed, depending on how you view it, their souls. This spell forced one's soul to fight mindlessly for him. When one dies, their soul simply transfers to another abomination made by Scaf and his tailors. The tailors were also enchanted by Scaf with the ability to create body parts from scratch. They then sewed them together, hence the name tailors, and fused them with a soul. Due to this, Scaf's army could never be truly defeated, unless Scaf is killed, and his spell broken.

I then began to wonder what happened to Mother and Fathers souls when Parla commanded, "You leave first thing tomorrow. I suggest you get some rest."

CHAPTER 16

I woke up naturally as the sun rose through my window, light seeping onto my face. I had to cover my eyes and slowly adjust to the bright light. A bowl of rabbit stew sat on the platter on my dresser. It instantly reminded me of my last meal with Mother and Father.

The stew was magnificent. Girthy carrots, juicy rabbit, and a plethora of other bits and pieces that I couldn't name. It was much better than Mother's. I thought back to Father insulting her cooking, and then throwing his spoon at her. It felt like yesterday. Yesterday couldn't be far enough away.

I finished the stew and took my normal steamy bath. I dressed in the typical toga and sandals given to me. They didn't feel comfortable at all. I almost missed my peasant clothes. Almost.

Priests and priestesses avoided looking at me as I passed them down the hall. I no longer felt above them. I regret treating that priestess with such disrespect before.

I joined Parla in his throne room. More guards were present than usual. Parla noted my entrance, "Ah, there you are. My guards shall lead you to General Starfli's war camp. I hope you find their company acceptable. If not, you're in charge. Order them around as you please." I nodded. Parla pushed, "Do you always need my permission to leave?" I stared at Parla. I didn't know the correct answer.

Parla sighed, then jokes, "Yes, yes you do. That was my way of telling you to go. Lighten up, you're only leading an army of militiamen and untrained warriors against the never-ending undead!" This wasn't very comforting.

I turned to leave. A handful of guards followed behind me down the palace steps. I wonder how many of them would walk back up again, if any at all. I counted seven men. Seven men who left their lives in my hands. Soon they'd join another 9,000, who entrusted me the same way. This scared me.

One of the guards spoke in a young, almost childish voice, "Do you know where we are headed, General Dylan?" General Dylan. I liked the sound of that, it felt meaningful. I responded, "Lead the way, I'm sorry, I don't know your name." the man, not much older than I, replied, "Remus, at your service." I intended to learn the name of each of my men over time. I didn't wish to treat them as meat, as there is more to a man than his muscles.

Remus took the lead, although he made sure not to get too far ahead of me. He led us through the cobbled street, which turned into paved dirt, which turned into trodden grass, and eventually, an unbeaten path. Houses became fewer and smaller as few went, along with people.

After a few hours of walking, a man from the back of the line in an older, gravelly, and stern voice asked, "General, may we stop for a moment? My old legs can't keep up with you young bucks." I turned to face the man. I couldn't see through his red, steel, helmet.

Parla's guards all wore armor in this fashion, and brandished either a spear and shield, shortsword and shield, or rarely, a double-sided ax. I asked, "What is your name?" The old man responded, "Clayton, General. I apologize-" I cut him off, "No need. At the next river, we will rest." Clayton nodded in appreciation and said, "Thank you, General." I turned back around and continued to walk behind Remus.

Sticking to my word, we stopped at the next stream. The men sat down against trees and sharpened their weapons. Remus took his helmet off and drank from the stream. He had long, smooth, blonde hair. His face was clean shaven, and he looked no older than 20. His green eyes matched the mossy floor of the forest.

A soldier I didn't know asked, "This way leads to Talithia, does it not?" Clayton answered, "No, opposite direction actually." The soldier quietly said, "Oh. Forgive me, I'm rather directionally challenged." Clayton laughed soft heartedly and assured, "No worry, it took a lifetime for me to understand what was where." The group was then silent, enjoying being still for a moment.

The woods were serene. Birds chirped and occasionally flew overhead, bringing life to the scene. A gray squirrel was climbing a tree, being mindful of our presence. The small stream trickled peacefully, going wherever gravity took it. I had never been this far from the city of Parlania, but I didn't mind it.

Rustling in the bushes to my left broke the atmosphere. It didn't sound like an animal scampering, but someone walking. Not just one, but a few. Remus quickly wiped his mouth dry and put his helmet on. Men put their sharpening stones away and brandished their steel. We hid behind trees so that whoever was coming our way would be met with a surprise. I called upon my forced ability.

I remembered that I forgot to ask Parla how my blood tentacles worked. I almost wonder if they weren't tied to my emotions. When I was angry, they seemed to work much better than when I was calm. I guess I could put that to the test soon, if the situation required it.

Chapter 17

Twigs and pinecones crunched under the oncoming footsteps as they neared. I looked at each soldier. None of them showed a sign of fright, or worry. It impressed me, as I was pretty much soiling myself.

Suddenly, one of my men jumped out from behind his shelter, and yelled, "Who goes there!" After realizing what he was faced with, he yelled to the rest of the group, "Resurrects! Ready yourself!"

I stepped out from behind the tree, and the other soldiers followed suit. When I first saw the Resurrect, I almost puked. I had heard they looked awful, but I didn't know they were this inhumane. Just like the stories, their limbs were held together with thick string. Dried pus and blood seeped from the sewing holes, along with any open wounds on their body. Their skin was an odd gray, with bulging blue veins. The few that had hair, had thin, scarce hair. They had solid blue eyes, which made it tricky to tell what they were looking at. They all used chipped, warped, even broken weapons. One of them had a sword that was snapped in half, having jagged edges for a tip.

My guards wasted no time, and charged at the enemy. I watched as Remus used his shield to block an oncoming throwing hatchet, and slice the torso of a skeletally thin male Resurrect. The monster's organs spilled out, but that didn't stop him. Remus shoved his sword into the Resurrects mouth as it went to bite him.

I joined the battle, not wanting to seem like a coward. I began by sprinting at a Resurrect holding a torch and a serrated dagger. He held his torch out in front of him to stop me from bull-rushing him.
    The first thing I tried was to steal his torch with my tentacles. It didn't work. I made what I thought to be eye contact with the dead man walking, but it wasn't for sure. I went to swing at the torch to cut it in half, but the Resurrect pulled it backwards. He then used his serrated knife to try and lunge at me, but I stopped it with my shield. I then used my sword to cut his hand off at the wrist. Twine connected to both his hand and wrist and chose sides to stay on, while pus and blood spilled from both. The Resurrect seemed although it felt no pain. Not a single wince, nor grunt.
    He once again stuck his torch out, warding me backwards. I looked to the side as Clayton skirmishes with a Resurrect, vitalizing his spear's ranged blade to keep himself at a safe distance from his enemy. I used my shield to push the torch backwards into the Resurect's face. When he tried to back away from his torch, I shoved my sword through him, lifted him up, and impaled him onto a tree. Unable to move, I held the flame to the monster's face. The smell of burning and rotting flesh invaded my nose. It was unpleasant, to say the least.
    I looked for a new target when I saw a massive Resurrect swing a gigantic steel bludgeon at one of my men. He ducked under it, and jabbed his spear into his stomach. The beast grabbed it with one hand, pulled it out,

and spiked it downwards. It embedded itself into the soldier's lower leg, coming out the other end, and sticking into the ground. Blood dribbled down his calf armor as he yelled in pain. The scream reverberated off of his helmet, making it sound like he was in an empty room. I ran over to save the man, but it was too late.

His fate sealed as the brute slammed his bludgeon downwards with both hands onto his head. His helmet caved in like a bowl, and pieces of his head blew out of each side. It looked as if someone had crushed a can of tomato paste. His body slumped, although his leg stayed upwards, thanks to his spear.

I continued to run at the monster. He saw me coming, and swung at me. Using my momentum, I slid on my knees under the attack. Before he could turn around, I jumped on his muscular back.

Using his shoulder stitchings like handles, that forced me to call my weapons back. I frantically began to pull and loosen them, trying to rip some too. The large Resurrect dropped his glorified bat and began to try and grab me off of his back.

Luckily, his muscles were too big, which didn't allow him to reach me. I tore multiple laces, and pulled them through. Warm bodily fluids oozed out of his holes and onto my hands. I disliked this greatly. His arms began to droop, until they both fell to the ground. I dropped from his back once his arms disconnected. I called upon my blade again, but another soldier claimed the kill before me, swinging his mighty ax through the monster's head.

I nodded my head in appreciation, although I was capable of finishing the fight myself. I looked around as a soldier drove his secondary dagger into a Resurrects torso, twisted it around, and began to carve him open. The Resurrect didn't die, so he continued to stab, slice, and retract his tiny weapon. The Resurect's front began to look like a tilled field. Soon, Clayton shoved his spear into the fiend's head, ending its life. Clayton informed, "You have to go for the head, son. Otherwise, they'll keep coming." I noticed that the dead Resurect's eyes no longer glowed blue, but instead looked normal, albeit extremely bloodshot.

Killing a Resurrect was much different than killing a man. You could tell they had nothing to live for, other than to kill. Knowing they could only be killed by their head being lost, and even then they came back endlessly, they fought as if mistakes had no consequence. It was an odd approach to a fight, but a slightly frightening one. I, too, would play a game recklessly if it meant I could try again forever.

Remus sat next to another fallen soldier, this one missing an arm. He removed the delimbed soldiers helmet to reveal a face that was beaten and bloody. He was breathing heavily. There was no chance he made it. This put our forces down to five guards, plus me. I counted twelve Resurrect bodies, which meant we fought outnumbered and only lost two. That's pretty good, if you ask me. I allowed my men time to dress wounds, bury the dead, and calm themselves. I chose to sit by the stream and wait patiently, and I was already at peace again.

Chapter 18

Once my men had gathered themselves, we set out once again. We had about an hour until sunset, which meant we were likely close to General Starfli and her camp. Two men in the back, one large with a heavy battle ax, the other skinnier with a longsword, were speaking of home. I picked up on the names Izac and Dame. They seemed to know each other pretty well, as they would occasionally insult the other's mother.

Clayton walked at my side, silently. Remus continued to lead the group, warning us of the rare hole or movement ahead. There was another soldier who walked behind us, yet in front of Izac and Dame. He was quiet, and had a relatively mysterious demeanor. I wasn't able to watch him fight, So I wasn't sure of his skill with his spear and shield. For some reason, I was eager to meet him, but I couldn't think of a way to make it minimally awkward. Maybe I'd get the chance to talk to him later when we set up camp for the night.

When the sun began to set below the horizon, and the shadows cast from the tree's became darker, we decided to bed down for the night. Izac and Dame left to gather firewood, Clayton and I started setting up a firepit, and Remus made sure the area was clear of Resurrects.

Clayton and I dug a shallow hole with our hands. I asked him, "Which one is Izac, and which one is Dame?" Clayton answered, "Big bastard is Dame, scrawny one is

Izac. They've served together for longer than I've known them. It's hard to separate them given their past. Watching them fight each other is extravagant, but it's even more amusing watching them fight alongside. I've never seen more passionate soldiers in all my time, and I'm getting old! From my experience, they're good boys, both of them." I had picked up on the friendship between the two. It was good that my guards had a more personal connection, that way they wouldn't become traitorous.

I asked, "What about Remus? He seems to be a great leader." Clayton's face sunk a little. He informed, "Remus is indeed an excellent leader, but only through trial by fire. He's gotten many men killed, but luckily, he screwed his head back on right. Remus doesn't show it, but he feels guilty for those that died under him. He won't talk about it, so I'd advise against asking him about it." I remarked, "Noted."

Clayton began to gather rocks for a small hearth while I put kindling in the center of the pit. After a few moments of silence, Clayton said, "I've been in the service since I was about your age. After a few years, I came back, and got married. My wife fell ill after two years of marriage, and passed." I could hear Clayton's discomfort in his voice. He clearly wasn't over his loss. He continued, "After she died, I enlisted in the royal guard. After a while, I was asked to rejoin Parla's army. I had nothing else to do, so now I'm here. I've fought my whole damn life, and I don't plan on stopping."

I said nothing to Clayton and asked him about the remaining soldier. Clayton shrugged and said, "Haven't served with him before. Seems awfully shy." This furthered my intrigue in the man. Who was he? Why was he here? Then, I realized I hadn't seen him in a long time. Before I could dwell on it for long, Izac and Dame returned, holding timber.

They threw the firewood into a pile on the side, and began to strike rocks against each other to start a fire. After some elbow grease and a bit of luck, they lit the leaves and twigs I had gathered. Before long, we had a steady fire going. Remus returned and said nothing, so I assumed he didn't find anyone. We all sat around the fire and exchanged stories.

It was pitch black out now, other than the slight illumination from the campfire. Smoke rose straight into the air, as there was no wind. Small ash particles flew into the night sky to join the stars, which slowly disappeared into the darkness. Leaves and branches made it tricky to stargaze, but I didn't mind. I was too busy listening to Izac tell Dame his mother had an unnatural sexual prowess to care about the sky.

Suddenly, leaves crackled under someone's feet. We all drew our weapons and stood up. I prepared for another Resurrect encounter, but was relieved when I saw it wasn't a threat.

The mystery man came bearing the gift of a small deer. A spear hole in the side suggested he had either thrown his weapon, or snuck up and stabbed it. Both circumstances were impressive. We all laughed and yelled in appreciation of the meal.

Izac gutted the deer and prepared the meat while Remus crafted a spit to roast it. Dame, Clayton, the unnamed man, and I sat around the fire, eagerly awaiting supper. Dame asked me in his deep, guttural voice, "Where do you originate from? There must be some reason Parla chose you." I didn't know how to answer the question. I couldn't tell them the truth, or they could lose faith in Parla. I also didn't want to lie, as I came to like these men in the short time I had known them.

I answered, "My parents died, and my brother is sick. Parla offered to heal my brother if I helped lead his army." I didn't lie, I only left out that Parla was responsible for my parents deaths, along with Devon's sickness. Dame nodded in sympathy and spun his tale. "I was abandoned by my mother as an infant. Izac's family found me on the street and took me in. Izac's grandparents took care of him, as both of his parents served at Parla's palace. I've always thought of him as a brother, other than the fact that I wouldn't pork my brother's mother." Dame made sure to say the last part louder, teasing Izac. Izac stuck his middle finger up to show he heard Dame. It made plenty of sense to me as to why Izac and Dame were so close. Devon was my brother via blood, but I still understand the bonds of brotherhood are the strongest there is.

Just as we ran out of things to talk about, Remus set up the spit. Izac came over and pretended to drop the meat directly in the fire. No one found this funny except him. We took turns spinning the deer over the flame. It proved to be more challenging than it seemed; the flesh was heavy. We all continued to introduce ourselves, all but the quiet man. He didn't even take his armor off like the rest of us, hiding his face. I paid no mind to the man, and continued to listen to Izac and Dame's hilarious banter.

    They were polar opposites, which made it weird to see them get along so well. Dame stood at least a full foot taller and wider than Izac. He had thick, shaggy, black hair and a full beard to match it. His brown eyes reminded me of Fall leaves. On the other hand, Izac was short and thin, with shiny, blonde hair. His face was shaved clean. His bright blue eyes reflected the fire in front of him, along with the flames of a prankster. You could tell he meant no harm in his actions, although he might unintentionally cause some at times.

    Dame prodded, "Oh please Izac, your mother only gets on her knees for two things: to pray, and to get mine." Izac retorted, "Speaking of, here's something you can get. How about fucked?" This was one of Izac's weaker comebacks, but it got a laugh nonetheless.

    Izac continued, "Mothers aside, who do we have to thank for this meal? I haven't caught your name yet, stranger." Everyone turned to the suited man. He took his helmet off to reveal a grisly sight.

    Horrible burns coated his face, which allowed for only patches of hair to grow. He was missing an eye, with a scar over it, and the other was green. The man said in a quiet voice, "They call me Panther. Don't mention the food, it was better than sitting around." Clayton eagerly asked, "How'd you kill it? You don't have a bow, so you did it with your spear, but how?"

    Panther answered monotony, "Took all my armor off to keep it from clinking. Followed its tracks for about a quarter mile before I saw it. No wind meant she couldn't smell me as easily. I hid in a kind of shrub I watched her eat a few feet away. After a few minutes, she came to my bush. That's when I stuck her." While it was impressive, his story telling skills were poor. No emotion was in his face. Panther just stared at the fire, entranced by its glow.

    We sat in the silence created by Panther's awkwardness. He put his helmet back on, and cleaned off his spear using heat from the fire and a cloth. While Panther might've been socially underdeveloped, he was clearly dangerous. I respected that, and nearly feared it.

    We shared a juicy, yet unseasoned, deer. For what it was, the meal was good. It didn't compare to smoked ham, but it would suffice. After piggishly stuffing ourselves, we talked about who would take watch, and when. I took the first watch to please the others.

Chapter 19

Dame woke me up, as he had the last watch. I sat up to see everyone suiting up in their armor. The fire was nothing but smolders now, with a sporadic crackle or pop. I stood up and stretched out. The ground wasn't the most comfortable, but I am also used to a cushy bed. I brushed the dirt and leaves off of my toga and mozied over to Remus.

Remus was just putting his helmet on when he noticed me and said, "We have about two hours until we get to General Starfli's camp. If we start now, we can be there before lunch." I replied, "Well, let's get a move on then."

After roughly two and a half hours, we arrived in an open plain. Red and black tents were set up, most likely to house troops and plan logistics. Men in armor littered the campground.

Some of them shot at targets, others sparing with wooden weapons. I was amazed; I had never seen so many people in one place. It worried me that there were even more enemy units than this. I felt uneasy about being in charge of this many men. I could get all of them killed, I could send a few home, or I could send many home. It was all up to me.

We were greeted by two men wearing armor that appeared much more grand than the others. They must rank higher in the military. They donned spears and round shields, along with black horse-hair fans on their heads. They didn't have face guards. Both of them had no defining features: no facial hair, brown eyes, average facial structure. They looked at if they were bred to be inconspicuous. The rightmost one directed, "Welcome to General Starfli's camp. She has ordered us to retrieve anyone entering the area." Remus nodded in compliance.

We were led to a tent bigger than the others. Two more soldiers stood by the entrance. When we neared, they opened the curtains for us.

Remus and I walked in side by side, with Clayton, Izac, and Dame in tow. Another two guards stood in the tent, protecting who I assumed to be General Starfli. When Starfli noticed us, she waved the guards out. We didn't realize she also meant my men when she said in a bold, passive-aggressive voice, "Everyone but Dylan, get moving boys." Remus shrugged and said, "Well, I guess we'll go make some friends then."

Once only Starfli and I were in the tent, I took a second to admire her physical qualities. She had long blonde hair, and was a tad shorter than me. She had deep blue eyes that if one wasn't careful, they could drown in as if it was a strong ocean current. She was surprisingly muscular compared to any other woman I'd ever seen.

Starfli scoffed and said, "When you're done gawking, we can start." I shook my head quickly, regaining my focus. I apologize, "Sorry, I- " Starfli cut me off, "I'm not worried about it, when you're the only woman in the area, you catch all kinds of looks. Just don't think I won't bust your ass like I would anyone else's." Starfli demanded respect with the way she talked, and I kind of liked it.

She continued, "Anyways, what do you know of the Resurrects? We'll start there. I've been told you've never had an encounter with one before?" I nodded and went to speak, but Starfli cut me off, "Okay then. Long story short, they don't stay dead for long. An infinite army against a small one is certain defeat, unless we find a way to permanently kill the bastards. Any idea how we could do that?" I began, "We could try and purge the tailor- " Starfli interrupted again, "Yes, yes the tailors. I would've already dispatched them if they weren't so well protected. Scaf knows they are the backbone of his army, so he keeps them near to him. Any other ideas?"

I thought for a second, but nothing came to mind. Starfli put both hands on her slim waist and sighed, "He could have sent someone with above average intelligence to help instead of another handful of soldiers." General Starfli turned around and continued, "I can't win His war if He doesn't give me what I need." I looked at the table between us. There was a map, along with little blocks and pins representing points of interest, troops, and even spies.

After studying the map a little, I noticed two things: We had a downhill disadvantage to Scaf's main city, and secondly, there was a body of water outside the city. Scaf's city had a sea on one side, with a river that ran through it.

"What if we battle upstream to push them back, then send ships behind the city to box them in. We could wait them out!", I suggested. Starfli looked at me with a cold, uninterested face. "Wait out the undying. Right.", she mocked.

Now that I thought about it, maybe it wasn't a good idea. I asked, "What if we continue to push into the city, rather than stopping and waiting?" Stafli angrily responded, "We don't have enough numbers for that. If Parla would just conscript a boy here and there, rather than sending me scraps from the bottom of his personal guard's barrel, we could do that." I could tell Starfli was agitated, so I said nothing.

She calmly stated, "It isn't your fault. I'm sure you're a fine fighter, but it is simply not enough." I inquired, "What if the boats are only manned, not full?" Starfli stood up straight and began to think. She humored me, "Keep going." I explained, "The boats could be manned just enough to function, and we could bluff about our numbers." Starfli countered, "And if they call our bluff? I'm sure Scaf has spies the same as us."

I answered, "We are on the water, it's an easy retreat. By the time we are busted, our-" Starfli interjected, "My. You mean my troops." I stuttered, "Y-yes, sure. By then, your troops will be close enough to attack with almost full numbers. I'm sure if you send out a messenger, Parla would even supply the sailors so that we, eh, you have unchanged numbers!" General Starfli now stood looking at the pieces on the table. She shuffled them

PAGE 74

around according to the plan, and rubbed her angular chin in a moment of deep thinking.

Starfli complimented, "I see why Parla chose you. I'll talk it over with my advisors and captains tonight. Dismissed." I turned to leave as I was told. Just as I was about to exit, Starfli said, "You might not be so bad after all." This gave an odd warmth, and not one fueled by rage, nor fighting. I'm not sure I knew what caused it, to be completely honest. One thing was for sure: I didn't mind it.

Chapter 20

After a while of asking strangers and making educated guesses, I found my group. We had been placed in a tent close to General Starfli's, probably because I was important to Parla, which made me a high priority. I didn't like that my personal worth was tied to another man, even if he was a God. Hopefully by the end of this escapade, I'll have made a name for myself.

Once I had found my men, it was near dusk. A massive plate of metal was struck, signifying that supper was ready. I hadn't eaten since last night, so I was starving.

Once I saw what supper was, I instantly lost my appetite. A bowl of an odd, chunky slop was handed to me, along with a slice of bread and a mug of water. Every other person ate the food, if it could be called that, without a problem. I seated myself between Clayton and Remus at a wooden table. The tables were seated outside, which meant any rain could ruin the meal. That is, if it wasn't already terrible enough.

Dame scarfed his food down, which didn't alarm me. A behemoth like him needed food. Izac took meager bites, testing the slop in front of him. Remus and Clayton also uneasily ate, but ate still.

I broke off a piece of bread and dipped it in the disgusting mixture. Luckily for me, the gruel had no flavor. It shared a consistency with brick mortar, but a taste with none. I ended up eating the whole bowl and the bread, then slammed the water. It wasn't good, but not as bad as I had predicted.

I burped loudly, wiping my face. Dame smirked and took it as a challenge. He took a massive swig of water and let out a horrifyingly deep belch. It sounded like the bellow of a demon. This caused the table to giggle like school children. Remus followed, and let out a very long burp. It didn't have an impressive tone, but I couldn't have matched its length. Izac tried to compete, but had trouble matching our pig-like skill.

After drinking all of his own water, Izac stole Clayton's and tried again. Clayton tried to object, but it was too late. Izac downed his water, and let out a tiny squeaking burp. It was a disappointment to its competitors. Clayton insulted, "You didn't just drink my water to shame yourself, did you?" Izac brushed it off, "Bah, fuck off. I didn't hear you, old man!" Clayton seemingly took this personally. He quickly stood up, and left the table. We all showed disapproval.

When Clayton was out of sight, we all expressed annoyance toward Izac. That was, until Clayton returned, rolling an entire barrel of water. He had rolled it all the way from the canteen to our table, just to prove a point.

Clayton lay down on the ground, put his mouth under the spigot, and opened the latch. After drinking for almost 15 straight seconds, he stood up, pounded his chest like an ape, and let out the roar of a lion. It was long, deep, and unprecedentedly loud. Once Clayton finished, the table looked at each other in amazement.

Never in my life did I think I would have heard a burp that impressive, let alone from an older fellow. We all burst out into gut-busting laughter. Remus wiped tears from his eyes, and I found it hard to stay sitting up. Clayton took a well-earned bow and provoked, "Now that you've heard me, would you like to try again, Izac?" Izac lowered his shoulders and head, then sadly answered, "No." This sowed another outrage of laughter from our table, and the surrounding tables, whose attention we stole.

I came to realize I enjoyed the company of these men more and more with each passing moment. Never had I ever fit in so well with a group like this before. It made me happy. Not a fake happiness caused by believing I held power, but one forged by new friendships. It would kill me if anything happened to these men.

Chapter 21

I woke up in a scratchy, uncomfortable cot. I had gotten the last pick, since I was stuck talking to General Starfli. I got the cot placed closest to the entrance, which meant the chilly air affected me the most. I had goosebumps up and down my arms from being cold. Without really knowing how I did it, instinctually, I sped my heart up so that blood circulated faster, keeping me warm. This meant I had to breathe a little deeper, but I'd rather that than being cold.

I was the first one awake out of the group. I didn't want to wake them, as they told me last night a bell would signal it was time to get up. I lay in bed, staring at the cloth ceiling. I hadn't even been to war yet, and it already terrified me. Not because I was afraid of dying, but because I didn't want anyone else to die. I swore mentally to protect my men, no matter the cost. We would massacre Scaf and his playthings, and return home together.

After mindlessly looking at the black and red tent-top for what felt like eternity, a loud, deep bonging noise echoed across the plains. It rang five times, just to make sure no bear in a thousand mile radius could possibly hibernate. I got out of bed in a lethargic manner, still not completely awake. I looked around the room to see Remus, Izac, Dame, and Clayton stretching out and waking up. Panther sat on the floor, suited in his armor, and sharpening his spear. I forgot all about him last night. I wonder where he wandered off to.

Before I could dwell on it for long, a high-ranking soldier pulled out curtains open, and looked at me. He said, "General Starfli needs you quickly, Sir Dylan." I took a long blink and nodded, showing I understood.

I was still wearing the same dirty toga from two days ago. I began to feel grimy again, but tried not to focus on it. I wondered where I could get a new set of clothes from around here while I walked over to Starfli's pitched abode.

Starfli stood around her logistics table with two other men. They seemed to be of nobility, rather than guards. Attention turned to me when I entered, although it quickly changed back to the table. Starfli said, "So it's settled. We have basic fishermen man these boats dressed as soldiers, which will hopefully trick Scaf into thinking that a water retreat isn't an option. We then split our forces equally and send one group up each side of the stream. I would keep them together, but it expands into a river, and even rapids in some areas. Once we reach Scaf's City, we fan out, blocking any land exits. Scaf won't hand his city over, so we are going to have to penetrate and kill his tailors as fast as we can. That will minimize our casualties, while also killing the Resurrects for good. Once it's possible, I'll send a group of my best men to dispatch Scaf."

I disagreed, "I'll go alone after Scaf. I know this isn't my war, but Scaf is my fight." Starfli thought for a moment, then agreed, "Fair enough. But don't fuck it up." It was nice to see that Starfli listened to my plan, then polished it up a little. I guess that sometimes, you just need an extra set of eyes to a situation.

    One of the men standing around the table said, "It's settled then. I'll return to Parlania and inform Parla of your plans. Give the sailors, say, four days to get into position?" Starfli agreed, "Four days from now, we will begin our land invasion at noon. That should put us at their walls come night. We can camp and evacuate any wounded along the way, then continue the next day." The remaining man agreed, "That works for me. I'll send for a few priests and doctors to set up camp here, that way they don't have a couple day walk to medical attention. It should save a few more lives." Starfli stood up straight, and crossed her arms, "So it's settled. I'll inform my commanders, who will inform the soldiers of our plans. Dismissed." I turned and left with the nobles.

    It was going to be a long four days.

Chapter 22

We passed three of the four days by playing cards, talking smack, and mingling with new faces. Panther never got involved in these situations, no matter how we coaxed him. Dame even offered to share Izac's mother with him if he played a few rounds of knucklebones.

On the morning of the fourth day, everyone was awake before the bell rang. Part of it was new soldiers having trouble sleeping, the others preparing early for conflict.

A set of red and black armor was set neatly at the foot of my cot, surely a gift from Starfli. It had black horse-hair on the top, replicating the high ranking commanders. I put the steel leggings on, then the plated boots. Clayton helped me put my backplate on as I connected it to my chestplate. I then put my greaves on. I carried my helmet; it was uncomfortable to wear. I'd put it on when I needed it.

Once the wake-up bell rang, every soldier left for an opening in the field. We separated into commanders and their soldiers. Half of us went on one side of the small stream, half on the other. Supposedly, the stream opened up into a river too wide for us to cross. We had to push the Resurrects back on each side of it, otherwise one side would have a clear path to Parlania.

I grouped up with my men near the front of the right side, although not so close to the front that we would all certainly perish. I thought of my promise to myself and my brothers, and planned to stick to it.

General Starfli rode to the front with two other men to address the group. She began, "I won't lie. A sizable amount of the men I look at now won't return to this camp again, nor to their families. For some of you, this is your last day here. For another few, tomorrow is the last. Now I ask, who here will lay down and die?"

Everyone chanted a mixture of, "Not me!", "Not if I have anything to say about it!", and other similar words. Starfli continued, "I didn't think so! For your wives, your sons and daughters, I ask you for one thing: your best! Let's show these undead pieces of shit what happens when you come after our home!" Starfli raised a fist in the air. Every man in Parlania's army cheered, thrusting their weapons into the sky.

One of the horsemen went on each side of the stream to lead an assault. Starfli fell to the rear of the left side. Although inspiring, General Starfli seemingly wasn't without the fear of death.

Once the sun peaked above us, the calvary pointed their swords forward, signaling it was time. We marched, most to our deaths. Not me.

Chapter 23

After what I guessed to be about 45 minutes, a tiny scouting camp came into view on the left side of the river. Once the left side got into position, Resurrects came out from their tents to oppose them, although few in numbers.

Archers readied their bows to support them, gathering at the shores of what was now a river 12 feet wide. The water ran quickly, and seemed deep enough to where one would have to swim across it. Careful not to give the undead pricks much time to gather themselves further, Starfli blew a hand-held horn to signal a charge. Archers from both sides let their arrows loose, raining ammunition on the Resurrects.

The arrows cast thin shadows on the ground that grew in size as they neared their target. Thwacking noises were made from a mixture of arrows and bodies hitting the ground. Parlanian soldiers clashed with the disorganized Resurect's frontline, creating the cacophonous sound of smashing steel.

There wasn't much my men and I could do but watch and cheer on our comrades, so that's what we did. It took about five minutes for the Parlanians to cut them down. We lost only two, maybe three men in the skirmish, which was good.

Once Starfli's side regathered themselves, we continued to march. The river continued to grow in size, until it came to a collection of short waterfalls, no more than three feet tall. The left side took longer than us to scale it, as they were slightly fatigued. Panther gave me his hand to help pull me up a ledge. I took it, and was surprised by his might. It's no wonder how he threw a spear hard enough to fell a deer. Once above the others with Panther, we spotted resistance.

On both sides of the river, roughly 2,000 armed Resurrects stood about 300 feet from us. They stood still, waiting for our mark to charge. It was odd that they waited for our attack. It would benefit them to run at us while some of our troops were still getting up the small ledge, but I wasn't about to complain about their poor tactics.

Once every man was ready on each side, Starfli blew her horn again. Us Parlanians sprinted towards the opposition, and they stood still, raising their shields to intercept us.

I watched Dame grab a Resurrect's shield and rip it from his hands effortlessly. Izac then ran at Dame, and Dame used the shield as a platform to toss him into the air. Izac slammed his daggers into the top of the Resurrects head as he came down. I had to admit, it was pretty badass.

I parried an oncoming sword with my own blood shield, then punched his chest. I turned my hand, then called upon my sword. Without even having to move, my sword formed inside of his stomach. I pulled upwards, fileting him. Stuck on his sternum, I held my shield horizontally and beat his face in. Blood sprayed in my eyes with each attack, but it absorbed into my iris'.

I dislodged my sword, and swung at another Resurrect, this one holding two long-handled hatchets. He jumped backwards to avoid it. Men around me tore apart the Resurrects, grunting and yelling the entire time. I had never felt so much pride, so much spirit, in one place before. It would've been inspiring, had they been doing it for the right person.

I stood still, allowing the Resurrect to attack me first. He was oddly scrawny. One would figure the tailors would use muscled body parts to make their warriors. He stood there, doing the same as I. An unfamiliar horn blew. It was deeper than Starfli's, and louder. The Resurrects retreated.

Before they could get out of range, archer commanders ordered, "Release!" A fleet of bronze-tipped arrows chased the fleeing cowards, culling those who couldn't run fast enough. With arrows embedded in their backs, numerous Resurrects toppled.

Once we regrouped again, the wounded were sent to the back of the army. They would be left here and picked up by medics to be treated, as planned. We continued to march forward, and were met with trees. At first there were a few, but it became much more dense as we went on. Soldiers cut brush that blocked their path, bobbing around trees.

I made sure to do a mental headcount of my men. I hadn't lost any, which made my shoulders feel ten pounds lighter. We pushed onward for a few hours, and the river quit growing at roughly 25 feet wide. Occasionally we would stumble upon a wounded Resurrect who couldn't keep up with their group. They put up nearly no fight as we finished them.

The forest came to an end within the next hour. We were met with the sight of stone walls well over 30 feet tall. While we couldn't see much past the walls, a few ceramic shingled roofs poked above the ramparts. Smoke from bonfires and torches sent smog across the sky. Scaf had a very impressive keep, but it would crumble anyways.

Starfli and her cavalry went to the front of each side and informed us that we would be camping tonight. This would give us the chance to rest, sharpen our weapons, and come up with siege tactics to penetrate the walls. We fanned out around the keep in a semicircle, shore to shore. Tomorrow, we'd be on the other side of these walls. That is, if they still stood.

CHAPTER 24

I woke up under a small shelter made with a few sticks to hold brush up so that I could have a place to sleep. Most others did this, although some decided to just sleep on the ground.

The sounds of marching feet caused me to crawl out of my homemade abode in a hurry, along with a few others. Before long, every Parlanian was awake, and looking at the same thing.

Resurrects stood in the same curved line shape we did, threatening to defend their home. Archers and catapults populated the stone ramparts, offering the foot soldiers support. At the back of the army, undead horses were mounted by equally-vitalized monsters. They had more soldiers than us, along with cavalry, which we had none of. Luckily, they didn't call our bluff with the ships.

They did not advance, as if to say they would defend what was theirs, but only if they had to. We got into battle formations. The middle of each army parted. Starfli came out from our side, and a Cloaked Man from the other. They met in the middle of the barren field and talked for a moment. No one could hear them, but I assumed it wasn't a surrender from either side.

Starfli stood in the back of the army, although the other two horsemen galloped to the middle. The Cloaked Man did the opposite. He led from the front, and His cavalry rested in the back. I'm sure that was demoralizing to more than a few men. I didn't let it get to my head.

Standing at the front of the line, Remus and Izac were at my sides. Dame, Clayton, and Panther stood at theirs. It felt like we were our own little army. Starfli's horn sounded first, shortly followed by a massive gong, signaling the charge.

The enemy cavalry ran out first, and the foot soldiers stayed in place. Our own cavalry didn't dare take a fight that pitted two against what looked like 100. Instead, we readied our shields. Those with spears went to the front and stepped on their roundels to create a sort of intercepting spike. Panther did this too, bracing for impact.

Our archers let loose on the horses, making sure to take their movement speed into consideration as they fired. A few men here and there were struck and died, but not all of them. A horse with different colors of skin stitched together slammed into Panther's spearhead and toppled over. Panther was hardly fazed by this. He retracted his spear, then turned the rider into a kebab.

Those without spears stood around, watching those with them do all of the heavy lifting. Once ten or so remained, our two riders joined the frontline. More of our men were dead on the field, but now that the cavalry were done, we could advance. We marched forward in unison. Once in range, the Resurrect archers let loose. Everyone crouched down and held their shield up to protect themselves.

The Resurect's infantry charged. We followed suit, yelling as loud as we possibly could. The invasion had begun.

Chapter 25

    I thought the frontlines crashing earlier was loud, but it was nothing compared to the booming smash of every Parlanian soldier and every Resurrect monster colliding at once.
    I was two rows behind the front of the attack, but quickly became a first row fighter as the men in front of me died. I watched as one was sliced open from his left shoulder to the right side of his waist. Another Parlanian was decapitated, and blood spurted from his neck, falling limp.
    All of this blood was driving me insane. I felt as if I was unstoppable. Whether on my side or not, every ounce of blood absorbed into my skin. I broke through armor with ease, stealing lives as fast as I could. I couldn't control myself, and I liked it. A Resurrect nicked my shoulder with a shortsword, but I didn't feel it. I tackled him, ripped his hand off that held his sword, then pummeled his head into a pulp with my bare fists. After only a few punches, I hear his skull crack, and then cave in. It was gorgeous. It was terrifying.
    We slowly pushed the Resurrects back slightly, although we had lost many, many men. We had to continue to advance, otherwise tailors would construct reinforcements. Catapults threw massive rocks, flattening multiple people. Fortunately, they took a few minutes to get ready. Once the catapults began to reload, the archers

from both sides shot. I don't know how it happend, but tentacles sprouted from my back. They came out of what felt like millions of numb papercuts. They snatched up as many enemy arrows as possible and threw them back. They did this without my direct command, it was almost as if it was a subconscious instinct.

Our archers massacred their ramparts, sending most back to wherever the souls gathered. Without me and my ability, I guarantee Parlania would've already lost.

I lost sight of my men, but didn't pay much mind to it. My only care was to murder. They could hold their own, besides, I can't focus on winning the war if I have to baby them. Deep down, I knew this contradicted the promise I made to myself, but I didn't care. My bloodlust was insatiable.

We pushed the Resurrects all the way back to the gate in a feat of impressive fighting resolve. A ram pounded into the keep's gate, causing it to splinter and rattle with each strike. Ladders were set up to scale the walls. The Cloaked Man from earlier jumped over the wall in a single bound. I knew that it had to be Scaf. To get to Him, I first had to get inside the keep.

Once soldiers made it to the top, they rotated the catapults to face towards the city. Archers finished preparing them, then fired sporadically into the metropolis. With a final crack, the main gate blew open, sending wood chunks flying.

We were inside the City of Scaf.

Chapter 26

My men and I were the first behind the wall. It was oddly pleasant, considering it was populated by Scaf's mangled zombies. Buildings were constructed with stone bricks, and tall torches illuminated the streets. Cobbled streets ran in between these buildings. I assumed they were rife with people, if they could be called that, during the day. It was a shame it had to crumble.

Now that I was inside of Scaf's city, I had to get inside of his house. It would be the biggest in the city, undoubtedly. Panther deeply yelled to me, "This way!", and motioned his hand to follow me. I stood puzzled and asked, "What? Why?" Panther ran to me and grabbed my hand. "What the hell are you doing?", I exclaimed. Panther explained, "I know where it is. The House of Scaf is a few minutes away from here, but we need to get there quickly!"

I had never heard Panther speak this much. I trusted him the least out of all my men, but I trusted him still. Remus yelled, "Clayton and I are taking some men to clean out the town! Show that son of a bitch why Parla is the God of Blood and Wrath!" I hardly heard them, and Dame even less when he hollered, "Izac and I are going to find the tailors, make sure they don't make any friends!" I threw a thumbs-up with my free hand.

Panther finally let go of my hand, but continued to sprint, trusting I'd follow him. We ran through the vacant roads, occasionally turning at corners. The entire place smelt of wet, rotting flesh. My nose was fighting its own war, fending off the foul odor. We took a left turn into a small guard. They stood at the bottom steps of a massive residence, which I assumed to be the House of Scaf.

They wasted no time in attacking us. There were maybe 10, but they were armed with heavy armor, tower shields, and thick broadswords. These Resurrects seemed bigger than the others, almost as if they were made using better body parts. Panther and I stopped running and got ready for a tilted battle.

My adrenaline rush had worn off, but that wouldn't stop me from opening a can of whoop-ass on these bastards. My forearms split, offering me a way to clear the streets.

They moved in a line, holding their shields together. Panther and I did the same, although we were much less formidable. Panther held his spear on the right side of his shield, and I rested my sword on the top of mine. We took slow steps forward, cautiously meeting the enemy line.

Just as we were about to make contact, three horsemen came barreling down the streets. Horse hooves clopped on the stone streets, announcing their presence. It was Starfli and her riders! I didn't need her to win this fight for me, but I wouldn't complain. We stopped and allowed the cavalry to break the line up.

Starfli used a long handled ax to cleave a soldier's head in half, carrying him with her a few steps. She yelled,

"Go! We can take care of them!" Panther threw his spear at a distracted Resurrect, plunging it into his back. He dashed forward, and body slammed into his handle to force it all the way through the Resurrect. He was careful not to lose his balance, and retrieved his weapon. Panther ordered, "Well? Hurry up, we don't have all day!"

Funnily enough, we did have it all day. The sun was partially hidden, rising behind the magnificent house made from a kind of scorched stone, almost as if soot and ash were gently brushed over it. It only had one story, but was very spacious.

I jogged up the pristine stairs, watching my feet to make sure I didn't trip. Panther slowed to a walk and entered the throne room. Following, the massive, dark, wooden doors closed behind us with a smash.

Chapter 27

The room was nearly empty, except for the scent of wine and berries. It was a nice augmentation from the outside aroma. A strip of blue carpet stretched from the entrance up to the throne that sat at the top of a small set of stairs. It was made of tightly compressed bones. In it sat a Cloaked Man. I couldn't see His face. I didn't need to; I already knew who It was.

Scaf muttered in an elderly, raspy voice, "Good job, Panther. You may take your armor off now." I froze as Panther undressed himself. His entire body was burned. Small patches of hair spread across him that were only covered by a loincloth. He tore away at the skin around his neck, revealing slice marks.

Scaf gruffly explained, "We melted him together, this one. Stitches would be too obvious, he couldn't spy for me. You're lucky that bitch Starfli wouldn't let him in on your plans, or this assault would have been squashed before it was even started." I couldn't take my eyes off of Panthers' toasted corporeal form. He had deceived me. Panther wasn't even a traitor; he never was on our side in the first place.

Panther raised his shield and spear again, but this time, it wasn't with me. It was against me. He didn't speak, or show any emotion.

My blood boiled, literally. I called upon my powers, and walked towards the spy. Scaf chuckled, "Do what you do best, boys. Kill." Panther approached me, matching my pace. He locked eye contact with me. I looked into a pit of nothingness. His eyes never moved, locked dead ahead, seemingly just placed into his skull.

    Panther attacked first, hurling his spear at me with the strength of an ox. I didn't dare try to block this with my shield. I had seen what happened to the targets he hit. Instead, I swiftly jumped to the side. His spear flew straight, sticking into the large, wooden doors. With my enemy unarmed, I struck.

    Panther used his shield to deflect a swipe from me, and punched me in the kidney. This stole my breath, and sent a shockwave of aches through me. He then pushed his shield against me, but I pushed back. Panther used all of his might to oppose me, but I refused to be bested. I had come this far, and I wouldn't leave without Scaf's head on my belt.

    My feet slid on the ground as Panther forced me backwards. I rolled off of the right side of his shield, and came out behind him as he stumbled forward. I took a slash at his back. His flesh tore open, and rotted, burnt skin slid loosely across his back. Blood leaked from this wound, and I felt extremely uncomfortable as it absorbed into me. Scaf said amused, "You don't think I know who sent you? Panther was an experiment. He was pumped full of bear blood. It also happened to make him incredibly stoic."

    Panther turned around quickly, backhanding me with his shield. This sent me soaring into the air, and then to the ground. I nailed my face off the floor, and my nose began to bleed. Scaf sat up and eagerly challenged, "If this is the best Parla has to offer, he's doomed!" I tried to stand up, but Panther kicked me in the chest.

As he went to kick me again, I wacked at his shin with my sword. It came clean off, spurting blood on the floor and onto me. I then smashed my shield into Panther's other shin, tripping him. He fell forward, but not before I rolled away from him.

I got to my feet, and cut his arm holding the shield off at his shoulder. Scaf made no noise. Panther on the other hand, grunted in discomfort. I backed off, giving him a chance to situate himself, or threaten me. Instead, he begged, "Do it. We don't want to be trapped here anymore. Please, please free us." I plunged my sword into Panther's upper spine, killing him.

Scaf sat still, but said, "You fight in a sloppy manner. It will take me no time to kill you." I turned to him and provoked, "Try it then! I won't show you the same mercy." Scaf chuckled again, "Sure, why not?" Scaf slowly stood up, and his cloak slid off.

Scaf revealed two extra sets of arms, and chalky, blue skin. He wore only pants, showing off his impressive musculature. You could see his veins through his skin, which replicated the color of the deepest, darkest waters. Scaf pointed out, "Notice how I haven't a single stitch on me? I've never been so much as nicked, boy." I was sick of people referring to me as "boy", I felt I had more valor than most grown men.

Scaf grabbed weaponry from behind his throne. For his upper two arms that sat on top of his shoulders, he equipped a glaive in each hand. In his middle arms, he held rectangular shields with a tiny hole at the bottom for his lower arms' weapons, which were shortswords. The handles and hilts of each of his armaments were made of bones, coated in a shiny silver.

I had never seen a monster like this before. I expected another undead man, not a six-armed beast. This was going to be fun.

Chapter 28

Scaf was unlike his army; He attacked first. He dug His glaives into the ground, using them to swing at me like an ape. With His shields up to protect himself, Scaf stuck His swords through the bottoms of his shields. As He flew down the small staircase, I braced behind my own shield. Scaf made impact upon my shields surface, and sent me backwards, almost halfway down his throne room's walkway.

Scaf wasted no time, throwing both of His glaives at me. Chains clinked against each other, tied to the hilt of the weapons and His arms. I turned sideways, narrowly evading the attack from each side. They stuck into the door behind me, right around Panther's own spear. Scaf wrapped the chains tighter around His hands, and pulled as hard as He could, pulling Himself into me.

He extended both of his legs into my face. I heard, and felt, my jaw shatter into hundreds of tiny pieces upon contact. I dropped to the floor, leaking blood out of the incisions Scaf's sandals cut into my face. I swiftly jumped back up as Scaf yanked His glaives out of the door. Before He could turn to me, I ran to tackle Him, intending to impale Him on the handle of Panther's embedded spear. Instead, Scaf used the wall to do an acrobatic backflip over me.

I was aiming low enough to miss Panther's spear, but not the door. I used my hands to stop myself from hitting them. Scaf tempted, "Pathetic. You were sent to kill Me?" I would've verbally retaliated, had my jawbone decided to show up to work today.

I turned back around to face my adversary. Scaf swung his glaive at my neck using His chains, almost like a whip. I ducked and grabbed the chain. This time, I wrapped it around my wrist, and pulled as hard as I could. Scaf stumbled forward, losing His balance. I then threw His own glaive at Him like a javelin. Scaf stuck His shield up just in time to stop the attack. While He was preoccupied with saving His life, I found another way to threaten it. I pulled Panther's spear out of the door, and threw that too. It planted itself into the left side of Scaf's waist.

Scaf looked up, and to my horror, smiled. "It's about damn time.", He approved. He used his shortsword to break the handle of the spear off. Deep gray blood slowly left the gouge, and crept across the floor to me.

Scaf threw His swords, which also had chains attached, to the left and right of my head. I was too smart to fall for this maneuver again. I grabbed each chain, and pulled down on them. Scaf used His glaives to stop himself from hitting the floor, propping up against them.

Scaf crossed his bottom arms, which pulled both of His swords together. I jumped, and stood, one foot on each blade. I leapt from them, down at Scaf.

Scaf crouched and used His shields to intercept me. I stood on those too, and used my own shield as a wedge in between them. I forced my wedge deeper, creating a small opening between the shields. Scaf stabbed His right-most glaive at me, trying to get me off of His shield. I dropped my right shoulder back to evade this assault. Once His upper arm retracted, I thrust my own weapon between the crack my shield made between His.

  My sword plunged into Scaf's flesh, although I'm not sure where. What I did know was that it was deep enough to require stitches. *"Take that, you snide prick."*, I thought. I would've said it, but an insult wasn't worth my own agony. Scaf groaned in pain, and shoved His shortswords through the holes in His shields. I hadn't realized He pulled them back to Him until it was much too late. The swords skimmed my right ankle, but stabbed vertically into my left knee. Scaf pulled His right sword back, and used it to break the left sword's chain loose. He then thrusted His shields forward, launching me off. I couldn't use both feet to secure a landing, nor could I move my right knee to kneel. Instead, I flopped onto my back.

  I observed the hole in Scaf's chest, right below His heart. Had I stabbed even slightly higher, this duel would've resolved. Instead, I was rendered nearly immobile. Scaf stood back up straight and unwrapped every one of his weapon's chains from his arms. He cast His shields to His side as He slowly approached.
Scaf commended, "You're more respectable than I initially gave you credit for. You've given Me not one, but two wounds that'll surely need stitching. I won't even burn them away like I did with Panther. I'll wear your attacks to

display your undeniable might. A warrior's death, you deserve it. Unfortunately, I'm better. I'll make sure to tell Parla his attempt with you was valiant. How does that sound?" I was sick of Scaf's smack talk.

I pulled the sword from my knee, screaming as I did. Rather than my blood leaving, Scaf's entered. I felt my face reconstruct, and my wounds heal. I corrected, "I'm not done yet, asshole."

Chapter 29

Scaf laughed, "Impressive trick. But, expected. Your friends may have taken out my tailors, but not My personal tailor. I anticipated a strong adversary, so I made sure to stow My own away. Come on out, you little shit."

A gross blob of gore slid across the floor from behind Scaf's throne. It had animal hair that stuck to it, and mangled organs were spread out inside of it. I had no idea how in the hell it stayed together, but I guess that's what magic does: the unexplainable. I couldn't even absorb it. A tiny bone needle exited its slimy body, and floated towards Scaf. I watched as it patched Scaf up, erasing my progress. It then cuts open the back of each of Scaf's arms and his legs. The tailor then broke off tiny pieces of itself, levitating into the openings. They forced their way into the gashes, inflating Scaf's muscles. He started by breathing heavily, and eventually grunted, and then yelled, which turned into uncomfortable wailing.

As what was left the tailor used thick, musty string to sew Scaf's cuts, He said through breaths, "It's only fair if I can use the dead to gain more power too, right? That's all that these tailors are, after all. I hand-select the most twisted, yet intelligent, souls. I then force that soul into random piles of bodies that are left in the wake of My army. They then are responsible for controlling souls from My Pool of Souls, and putting them into bodies that they construct. They build these bodies using the magic I bestow in them, which is to infinitely create any biological matter. I'm certain these souls want to leave, but I care not. Without them, I'd be just another man."

    What Scaf did was horrific, but not unlike what I did myself. I now understood why Panther wanted me to kill Scaf, but why he still fought me. If Panther killed me, Scaf would treat him well. If I killed him, but Scaf killed me, Panther's soul would be treated poorly. If I killed them both, Panther, along with thousands of others, would finally be able to rest.

    Once the tailor was done, it sank back behind Scaf's throne. Scaf had grown at least three inches in height, and His muscles now looked as if they would explode and escape His skin. I could tell it was uncomfortable, yet empowering.

    Scaf challenged, "Well, we aren't done, are we?"

Chapter 30

 I readied my weapons, but there was something different this time. I felt as if I had another set of hands that were disconnected from myself physically, but not mentally. I couldn't put it into words, other than ethereal. Scaf walked forward slowly, intimidatingly. Once He was about ten feet from me, an unexplainable force came over me.

 Tentacles shot from my back. They weren't like the ones from before; they heeded my call. One wrapped around Scaf's top right arm as He went to punch me. Scaf then punched at me with every arm in a frantic, sporadic order. I grabbed each of them, halting His attacks.

 I pulled the tentacles tight, forcing Scaf's limbs to be fully extended. A tentacle binded around His ankles, restricting His movement. In a testament of strength, Scaf pulled against them with each arm at once, tearing through them. I had a short time window to make something of this.

 I sent another tentacle out to tie two of His left arms together, then strung them above His head, revealing the area His kidneys should reside in. I shoved my blade as deep as I could inside, extending it, leaving the tip protruding out of the other end of Scaf.

 Scaf didn't even care that I made a sheath out of Him. Instead of reacting, Scaf used His newly loosened lower left arm to grab my calf and raise me into the air, while forcing me to pull my sword out of Him.

 Scaf threatened, "Die fast, or slowly. I will give you this option once." I cut His arm off at the elbow, which dropped me. Scaf swung at me from every possible direction again. My shield was useless, so I replaced it with another sword, replicating the one in my right hand. I used my two swords to dice each of His arms. Hands, forearms, even biceps dropped to the floor making a wet, meaty slap.

 Scaf seethed, "So be it." The tailor sent out gobs of flesh, creating new arms for Scaf, equally buff. Blood climbed my legs and entered through my nostrils. It felt kind of disgusting.

 If I wanted to make any progress in Scaf, I would have to kill that damned tailor. I sent out two tentacles around him to try and apprehend the tailor, but Scaf reached out and grabbed them both. He then swung them around His head like a tunic at a drinking party, sending me into airborne circles. The room spun, until Scaf let me go.

 I blew a hole through the massive wooden doors, sending a rain of splinters everywhere. I hit the cobbled ground, bounced back some more, and hit it again. Everything on me was scuffed up, and little stone pebbles lodged into my skin, cultivating a burning and stinging sensation.

 A shadow was cast down from the sun, hitting the peaked tip of the House of Scaf. When I struggled to stand, light shone in my eyes. I used my sword to block out the sun, only for Scaf to pick me up by my raised arm.

He used His three right-side arms to punch me in the liver, repeatedly. He grabbed my other arm, held it up, and proceeded to beat on my other side. I felt my insides bruising, busting open even. Blood spurted from my mouth and nose as it filled my throat. It reminded me of Devon's coughing fits.

I took the beating, as there was nothing I could do about it. After Scaf decided He was bored with this, He dropped me. Mid-air, He punted me like a ball. This stole the breath from my lungs.

I hit a house's exterior wall this time, but I wasn't kicked hard enough to go through it. I slumped against the building and tried to regain my warrior mentality. Scaf walked to me again, picked me up by the throat, and held me against the hovel.

I tried to slice at Scaf, but He then grabbed my arms and legs. Tentacles wrapped around His throat. I felt my face swell while I watched Scaf mimic. I then tried to pick Him up using my tentacle, to no avail. My lungs felt as if they were filled with molten lava. My tentacle reefed backwards of Scaf, trying to pull Him and myself away from the wall. Nothing would work. My vision faded in and out, the intervals increasing each time.

A familiar, massive ax lopped Scaf's head off. I fell as He did, and lay in a growing puddle of His murky blood. I couldn't make out my savior, or who accompanied him, but they felt amicable.

Chapter 31

When I came to, I recognized Dame's deep voice. "Get up, you aren't done yet!", Dame pushed, "The others are going after the last tailor up there. Izac and I are here to hold him off until then!" I groggily asked, "Ho-how do you know there's a tailor?" Dame responded, "That over there tells me there is another one." Izac prodded, "Well? Get up!" Dame insulted, "He's worn out, much like me after a bout with your mother. Leave him be."

I regathered my senses on the hard ground, trying to fight through my pain. They had pulled me into the middle of the street, and I didn't even realize. I looked over to Scaf's body to see what Dame was talking about. His head was being rebuilt, reviving Him. Stitches attached the final product, giving Him the true Resurrect touch.

I fought to stand again, but couldn't. I watched as Dame and Izac took turns evading blows from Scaf, cutting into him. Izac's daggers did almost nothing to Scaf, other than distract Him so that Dame could slam his mighty ax into Him, carving out large chunks of flesh. This hardly slowed Scaf, as anything they took was reconstructed instantaneously.

Scaf quickly tired from this and grabbed Izac and Dame's weapons by the blade. The ax blew Scaf's hand into millions of fleshy bits, but rendered Izac stuck. Izac sawed away at his restraints, but his tiny knives did little.

Scaf grabbed Izac's left leg and right arm, lifting him. Dame tried to cut Izac free, but Scaf used all four remaining arms to grab Dame's ax's handle, stopping it.

    Izac began to scream in agony as Scaf pulled on his limbs. I heard his bones and joints disconnect, and his tissues tear. Dame pulled his ax back, and swung once more, but was halted again.

    This lit a fire in me. No one would kill my brothers, not even a God. I waveringly stood up, and unsteadily sprinted towards Scaf. I used both swords to cut into His gullet, slopping Scaf's organs into the street. I ripped them apart, just as He was doing to Izac. Izac continued to scream, until his leg came loose from his body.

    Warm blood squirted down onto my back, and on Dame's ax. Scaf dropped Izac as he howled, cried, in miserable, immeasurable pain. Dame shouted, "You son of a bitch! I'll fucking kill you!" I left Dame to his revenge. After what just happened, he could hold his own.

    I ducked under Scaf's arms, and over to Izac. I drug him away from the fight, and took all of his armor off. I expected to see bone coming out of his rough amputation, but that seemed to have come out with the other half of his leg. I put both hands on it, commanding the blood to stay inside. I reassured Izac, "You'll be okay, just hang in there." Izac said through strained, seething breaths, "I might be, but what about Dame?" Izac's eyes were shut tightly to help deal with the pain, so he couldn't see for himself.

I looked over to see that Dame had planted his ax vertically into Scaf's spine, but his spinal cord simply wove around it, trapping the weapon. Dame was now fighting with his hands, breaking Scaf's arms rather than cutting them off. I picked up on something monumental to the fight. Scaf's arms weren't healing! Remus and Clayton must've gotten ahold of that tailor!

Dame ducked a left hook, then shoved his arm into Scaf's stomach. Scaf stopped moving. Dame reached around, mixing the organs I had once pulled out, but the tailor had replaced. He pulled out Scaf's small intestine, and yanked, tearing a segment out. A gross slop spewed from each end of the tubing, splattering onto the street.

Scaf didn't know what to do, other than to stare into Dame's eyes, and cryptically warn, "A God's plaything and his band of mortals, forever cursed via killing Me. Enjoy not Parla's wrath, but true wrath. The wrath of a broken Mother."

Dame grasped Scaf's throat, sinking his fingers deep, and tore it out.

Chapter 32

Scaf's body lay in the street, His blood painting the cobblestone road, running between the cracks. Dame dropped to his knees, holding the gory chunk he tore from Scaf tightly, crushing it in his hands. He was breathing heavily, as anyone would after a fight like that. I couldn't have done it without my crew.

Remus and Clayton ran out of the building, ready to fight, but saw Scaf. Remus then saw Izac, and ran towards him. Swords still clanged and screams continued to echo from the battle behind us. Shortly, we all surrounded Izac. He wouldn't talk. Maybe he couldn't. His bleeding would persist if I left, so I commanded the others to go get help. The medics couldn't be far behind our army. Dame refused, and I didn't try to convince him.

"Turns out I won't be racing drunks for cheap coins anymore.", Izac lazily joked. Dame didn't find it funny, instead he just stared at his missing leg and apprehensively questioned, "How are you going to fight? You won't be able to walk anymore." Izac said, "Well clearly, but I'm not worried about that now. I'll get back to Parlania and get help, but you have to promise me you'll do the same." Dame couldn't shake his worries, and nodded.

The clashing of swords died out, and cheering began. Medics flew down the street on horseback, followed by Starfli. Medics surrounded Izac, wrapped his leg up, and put it in a tourniquet. Once his leg was covered, I let go of Izac's stump. Dame and I watched as they carried our friend away. Guilt fell over me, but before I could dwell on it, Starfli approached as the medics dispersed.

"Well? I didn't fuck it up.", I said. Starfli firmly responded, "I know you wouldn't fuck it up, otherwise I wouldn't have let you go after Him. I'm a general, Dylan. I don't take risks." It was a compliment, even if it didn't feel like it. Starfli congratulated, "Good job. I couldn't have killed Him myself." I looked over at Dame, still staring into space, and said, "I didn't do it myself." Starfli looked at Dame and concluded, "I see. We'll be plundering goods and regrouping in about an hour. Collect yourselves, and be there." I gave a small nod, and Starfli rode her horse back to the army.

"You hear her, Dame?" I asked. Dame didn't respond. I put a hand on Dame's shoulder and reassured, "There wasn't anything you could've done." Dame solemnly replied, "I know. That's why it hurts so bad." I related to that more than Dame would ever know. "I'm going to go rifle through Scaf's shit, want to come with?" Dame monotony replied, "No"

I left Dame to his thoughts. Sometimes, you have to just leave a man with himself.

Chapter 33

I walked past Scaf's lifeless body. The sight was intoxicating. I could only imagine the size of the statue that Parlanians would build for me. I kicked the door's remains out of my way, and stepped up to the throne room's entrance again. This time, it was my house, not Scaf's.

I walked down the center aisle, past Panther. I had kept my promise to him. I sat in Scaf's large, bone throne. Suddenly, Scaf's blood climbed the stone tiles and coursed through the throne, almost like a ritual. The flow entered through my feet, forcing itself into circulation. I could feel my heart accelerating. The blood of a God was thicker, more bountiful than a mortal's. I watched, and felt, as my veins ran darker than normal. My head nodded back in pleasure. I may not have killed Scaf myself, but I alone would benefit. Maybe I should hire others to do my work more often. Dame was my friend, surely he wouldn't mind.

Once Scaf was a part of me, I took a moment to appreciate my hastened blood-flow. It undoubtedly raised my internal temperature, making me pleasantly warm inside. I wonder what the blood of other Gods felt like?

I stood up, regaining my focus. I walked behind the throne to Scaf's actual home. His residence was much different than Parla's. He had no room for guests, no extravagant kitchens. It was almost as if Scaf was a modest ruler.

Upon entering Scaf's room, I noticed a few things. First, the blue color scheme continued. Second, Scaf had no taste in art, unlike Parla. Rather than paintings of grand scenes, Scaf hung abstract art on the walls. Small sculptures with unique geometry sat atop his dresser and shelves, further worsening his palette.

His bed sat in the corner of his room, not nearly as big as mine. All of his furniture was made from bones, which gave off a very foreboding presence.

I began with Scaf's dresser. He had cloaks, all the same design, in every single drawer. How many of the same garment could one own, before they had enough? I pulled every cloak out, searching for hidden compartments.

To my surprise, I found nothing but clothing and jewelry. I searched under the dresser, behind paintings, shook vases, yet was left empty handed. That was, until I looked under Scaf's bed.

A tiny box made from the same scorched stone the house sat alone, tempting me. I grabbed it, and opened it. There was a deep blue gem with no real shape. One side was smooth, the others having jagged edges. I wasn't sure what it was, but I pocketed it. I put the empty container back, stood up, and concluded my disappointing search.

Chapter 34

Following the sounds of cheering and laughter, I found myself with the army by the docks. The sun was setting over the horizon, painting a brilliant color display across the sky, which the sea gracefully mimicked. Scavenging ravens slewed around clouds of smog to find amalgamated corpses to feast upon. Gargantuan bonfires illuminated the night, spitroasting game the ships had brought with them in the event of victory. Soldiers congregated with their friends, elated to see eachother alive. If one was able to push the cost aside, the sight might've been beautiful.

I eventually stumbled upon my men, asking random people for directions. Everyone had their helmets off, a sign of feeling safe. Well, for everyone other than Dame. Dame sulked, sitting atop a barrel. He seemed to still be deep in thought, or perhaps even frozen in the exact opposite.

Remus and Clayton sat on the docks, their legs swung over the edge. They seemed to be talking, but I couldn't hear what they were saying. Our group felt solemn, broken, even. I didn't have to share the news of Panther, as I'm sure they saw his body while they were going after Scaf's tailor.

I grabbed a slab of salmon, sitting next to my comrades. I was greeted with warm smiles, yet hurting eyes, similar to those of a stray dog. The silence bonded us furthermore. We simply ate and stared off into the vast sea, wondering when it ended; not only the water, but the wars raging around, and inside of ourselves.

I couldn't help but feel as though I could've done something to help Izac. While I might have saved him, I wouldn't have had to if I simply kept him out of harm's way. How is his absence going to affect Dame's fighting? How about the morale of the group as a whole? The bond of brotherhood through combat wasn't one that could be replaced, nor replicated.

As we finished our meals, we set the empty plates behind us. Not killing our serenity, we continued to watch the sun sink below the water, its light submerging with it. Once a few minutes, which felt like days, passed, the only light was that of torches and embers from pyres.

Clayton was the first to revive the dead air. "They're putting us on the ships, then taking us back to some fishing village. Faster than walking." Remus and I sat quietly, although still acknowledging this information.

Once the mass was done eating, we were ordered by polemarches to board the boats. I clung close to my band, careful not to be separated. We were put onto a boat with roughly 100 others. This left minimal breathing room, but we managed. Once our ship was full, we pulled away from the dock, opening a spot for the next convoy.

The boat creaked as it meandered with the wind, gliding across the abyssal waters. Everything outside of our vessel was pitch black. It was a cloud-covered night, meaning not a single star could shine through to us, not even the Moon.

All we had for light were a few lanterns hung around, which wasn't much. We had to sleep in our heavy, firm armor, as there wasn't enough room to store it. It was hard and uncomfortable, but not a soul cared. We had fought our hearts out, which would leave any man in dire need of rest. I propped myself up on the wall to the captains quarters, right under an oil lantern. Bugs circled the light, creating an annoying hum. It didn't take long for me to fade off into slumber, the boat easily rocking me asleep.

CHAPTER 35

I woke up to a flash of light, which split the blackened sky open. From the lightning's incision, rain poured down. It took mere seconds for every one of us to be drenched, our armor squeaking with every movement.

It didn't take long for every man to get on their feet. We clung on to anything and everything to stay on the boat. The tiny fishing vessel shook violently as it made contact with high waves that threw ice cold water onto the deck. Lanterns flew off of their hanging hooks into the bottomless sea, rendering us blind. White lightning crackled above us, offering sporadic and unreliable light.

I grabbed onto the railing of the deck, along with multiple other men. There was nothing laying on the deck; every loose item was now sinking below us. In a sudden flash, a man next to me flew over the railing due to a wave crashing against the hull. He screamed for only a few seconds, stopping once his voice was lost below the surface. Those around me began to get frantic, fighting each other for room on handles.

A few men tried to take their gauntlets off to get a better grip on their safeguards, but would often be fed to the fish as they let go. I couldn't tell who was where, or even what was even really happening. The only thing I could do was hold on for dear life. I was freezing cold, even with my heart rate accelerated.

Just when I thought it couldn't get any worse, I saw spiraling beings leak from the spread clouds. With the arrival of serpentine dragons, one thing was made clear: this was Helana's doing. The lightning, rain, now serpent-like dragons, She had to have been enraged. Suddenly, Scaf's last words made sense.

Powerful gusts of wind echoed around me, undoubtedly due to the serpentines nearing us. I had never seen a serpentine, and wished I never had. They were long and linky, moving in circles and loops. They had smaller wings that ran down their backs, with two arms used for offensive purposes. Their scales were said to be impenetrable, leaving them nearly invincible. It was hard to see where they were, so no one could even attempt to avoid getting snatched up by their clawed hands.

I felt the outside of a massive hand harshly brush against me, stealing the soldier nearest to me. I heard as the serpentine's claw punctured his armor, hooking him through what I'd assume to be his chest cavity. I don't know which fate would be worse: being torn apart and eaten by one of them, or thrown into the blackened depths, wounded, to drown. Neither sounded preferable.

Those that drew their weapons were flung overboard, as they weren't able to hold on tight enough. We were being utterly massacred, and there wasn't a solution in sight. All we could do was accept our grueling deaths.

I watched through lightning strikes as a serpentine rammed itself into another boat's hull, splitting it wide open. Men poured from it into the sea, forever lost. A few hours ago we were all celebrating about being able to return to our families. Now, it was certain none of us would.

In a split second, lightning crashed into our boat's mast, blowing it apart, sending pieces of flaming timber everywhere. We no longer could use the wind to move. The boat began to lower closer to the water level, meaning there must've been a puncture in the hull, or maybe we had too much weight from the water sloshing around on the deck. It didn't matter how it happened, what mattered is that we were capsizing.

The water raised itself to the railing. People around me started screaming for it to stop, and for the aid of loved ones. A few tried to climb to higher points on the ship, only to be carried away into the night by serpentines.

There really didn't seem to be a way out of this one. I was going to die.

Chapter 36

A hand grabbed me around the waist, tearing me from the sinking ship. My heart rate was now out of my control. Shaken to the core, through flashes of light I saw myself getting further and further away from the ocean.

The bird's eye view looked even worse than ground level. Not a single fishing boat had survived. The few that were still above water had serpentines picking people off of them, sustaining severe damage. It was odd that the serpentine holding me hadn't tried to eat me already, nor rip me to shreds. We rose higher and higher into the night, until I couldn't make out any of the shapes below me.

Suddenly, I emerged above an opening in the rolling clouds. I saw something I could never forget. It was gorgeous.

A city sat atop the clouds, just like I was told as a child. Serpentines, wyverns, and dragons flew gracefully over the tall buildings. Every structure stood well over 500 feet tall, all with a glow in their windows. They were constructed from a sort of deep purple gemstone, which was incredibly smooth. Now that we were above the clouds, I could see the stars. Although I was thousands of feet from the ground, they still seemed so small, so far away. There was a full moon that lit the streets, which were made from deep, black clouds. I was in the lightning-infested clouds of Syvene, home of Helena and Her airborne reptiles.

The serpentine let go of me, quite a ways away from the clouds. I screamed as I plummeted towards the dark clouds, fearing the harsh contact. I landed pleasantly. It turned out that the clouds had a sort of squish, yet crunch to them. They felt as if snow could be a fuzzy blanket. My ankles sank below the clouds, the rest of me above them. From the ground, the infrastructure looked impossibly tall.

Before I could ponder why I was alive or why I was here, I was met by humanoid creatures. They had thick scales, ranging from orange, green, some even black. They didn't have wings like the other dragonkind. These seemed to be the normal civilians here.

Before I could do anything, they kept me at a distance using spears made from sheer lightning. Their glow reflected off of the cloud tops. I didn't know what to do, nor say, so I didn't take any initiative. They circled me. Then, once I was surrounded, the ones in front of me got behind me. I looked backwards, only to see their spear tips were getting closer. I walked forward, avoiding being zapped.

After being paraded around the streets at spear point, I was ushered into a skyscraper, significantly larger than the others. Dragonkind circled this one, almost like they were protecting it. Intuition told me this was Helena's residence. That meant I had been kidnapped, while every other person on the ships were dead.

To my surprise, Dame, Clayton, and Remus were already together, also being guarded. This was a massive relief. If they had all died, I'm not sure I could've continued with Parla's deal. We were then forced into a circle made by the guards, grouped together.

The bottom floor of the building was circular, and quite big. There was a staircase that wrapped around the outside of the room, which led to the ceiling. There was another set of stairs that led to a sort of bannister, with a throne made from the same material everything else was constructed from. The only difference was that lightning seemed to flicker inside of it. The throne sat empty, which was odd.

We stood still and silent. Not sure what would get us killed, we simply did nothing. A few minutes passed before She came down. She walked the outside of the room, around us, then took Her seat on Her throne.

"Godslayers, that's what they're calling you here. I call you fools.", Helena mocked.

Chapter 37

Similar to the other draconic humanoids, Helena donned thick scales, only a deep purple, whereas no other dragon did. It resembled the material that everything seemed to be made out of. She was rather tall, although with curvature that was easy on the eyes. She also didn't seem to have any wings or claws, but Gods could be deceiving.

Helena continued in a near seductive tone, "You know what you've done, and you know why you're here. I won't waste anyone's time. What I can tell you is that you'll regret your actions deeply. You know what to do with them." Helena signaled for us to be taken away. It was curious as to why She was allowing us to keep our belongings.

My men and I were taken to a large cage with a hook on the top. It was oddly spacious for a jail cell, and even weirder that we were being kept together. Something didn't feel right.

Once we were inside of the square holding cell, a dragon covered in armor swooped down, the gust of its wings almost enough to knock me over. I couldn't see it too well due to the solid gemstone roof above me. The guards tied thick chains to a loop on the bottom of the dragon's armor, then to our cage. I was able to catch a glimpse of a rider who sat atop the dragon. They had the same armor as everyone else, and donned a war maul made from lightning.

    Once we were connected to the beast, it took off. It was made apparent why nothing was taken from us: we couldn't escape this. We weren't even chained. The bars were close enough together so that we couldn't try to jump to our deaths.

    By now the sun was starting to rise over the clouds. As the light shone upon the deep purple material, its color began to transmogrify. It ate the sunlight up and changed into a light, brilliant blue. The clouds reverted to their normal, inviting white state. Our cage, even the dragon's armor changed. It really was a splendid sight. Syvene was a very aesthetically pleasing place to be. I hope Parla didn't want to burn this, too.

    The first thing everyone did was take their suits off. After wearing them for so long, it sent relief throughout my body to stretch. Remus then repeatedly, angrily, threw his helmet against the cage's walls.

    Clayton calmly, yet firmly stated, "That won't help us, son. Let's sit down, cool off, and think rationally." Remus stopped throwing his helmet, and held it close to his chest as he dropped to his knees and broke. "I-I did it again-n!", Remus yelled, choking back tears, "I thought t-this time would be different, b-but no!" Clayton tried to cut Remus off, but was yelled over. "It doesn't matter who I go into battle with, they all end up d-dead! And I don't! It isn't f-fair!"

Clayton stood up and walked over to Remus, setting his hand on his shoulder. In the manner of a grandfather teaching his grandchildren a valuable life lesson, he said, "Son, you haven't failed anyo-" Remus turned around and screamed in his face, crying, tears and snot running a river down his face, "And what do you know? How much of your brother's blood is on your hands?" Clayton, not taking this disrespect, yelled back, "Brothers? Son, my own wife's blood is on my hands! Do you know what that's like? To have a sickness tear someone from you because you can't afford the doctors? Killing innocent men for corporate greed, just so she can hold on a little longer? Watching her die slowly, painfully in front of you? The same woman I swore to protect! You don't ever get to tell me what I haven't lost, boy!"

A single tear rolled down Clayton's cheek, its weight matching Remus's handful. Remus seemed to be at a loss for words. All he could do was stand still, staring into the soldier's eyes he himself also had. Clayton embraced Remus in what I couldn't describe with any other word than the love of a family member. Remus stood there, accepting the hug, still quietly sobbing.

"We've all seen and done evil, evil things, son. What matters is that we're here now, living in their honor. Don't waste the chance to make those that have fallen at your side proud.", Clayton softly advised. Clayton let go of Remus, and went back to his corner, sitting down. He continued, "We aren't dying here. I've come much too far to die suspended next to a dragon's pecker."

CHAPTER 38

We sat together, all contemplating how we could make our escape. Remus still had his sword, although Dame and Clayton had lost their weapons. The only reason Remus's sword remained intact was due to having a leather clasp that held it in its sheath. We all had our armor in a pile that slid around the room, but that didn't do us much good. We could fit our arms through the gaps in the gate, but nothing else. The cage was suspended low enough so that we couldn't reach the dragon. Occasionally, we would pass another dragon carrying prisoners, some of them dead.

Dame silently stood up and stuck his hand out to Remus. Knowing what he wanted, Remus handed Dame his sword. The giant then took his helmet and beat chunks off of the sword. Remus hastily tried to grab his blade back, but Dame pulled it away and stared at him, notioning him to trust the process.

Dame continued to break incremental pieces from the blade. Once one side of the sword was done, he spit as much as he possibly could on one of his shoulder plates. Using his armor as a whetstone, Dame sharpened the improvised serration. It was interesting how none of us had to say a word, but we all knew each other's exact thoughts.

Dame then put one of his gauntlets back on so he could push on the unbroken side of the blade, and began to saw away at the crystal bars. I was impressed by this intuition, as all of mine fell short. The only thought I had was to kill the dragon with my tentacles. But, even if I knew how to control them, we would then be sent into a free-fall to our deaths.

It took hours before Dame made any progress. He had to resharpen the sword multiple times, asking us to spit on his shoulder plate, as his mouth was completely dry. White cracks flowed across the bar he was breaking, showing that he was slowly, but surely, getting through.

Once the sun peaked in the sky, he roughly sat down, dropping everything he was holding, taking his gauntlet off. His hair was drenched with sweat, which rolled in thick beads down his face. Remus then stood up, took the sword, and put his own gauntlet on. He continued where Dame left off, gliding his destroyed blade over the bar.

It started to rain again, which was nothing shy of a cruel joke. The dragon's size kept us from the water, meaning we couldn't try to drink any. Our helmets wouldn't fit through the bars to collect any, and our arms were too short to reach out and gather some.

Once Remus was completely worn, he handed the sword to me. I did exactly as they did. The blade's bumps made it awkward to cut with, as it moved in and out from the gate, meaning I had to keep constant extreme pressure on the back of the sword. While I worked, Dame and Remus slept. Clayton watched outside of the cage, wondering if he'd ever leave it.

The sun sank below the horizon once again. As shadows cast across our cage, it turned back into the deep purple we originally saw. I was about halfway through the bar when I physically couldn't continue. My arms burned like never before, and I could feel the thick sheen of sweat on my skin. I limply handed the sword to Clayton, then laid down on the hard floor. I took my gauntlet off, then fell asleep myself.

*   *   *

Another full day had passed before we broke through the bar. We were all dehydrated and hungry, although not starving. Clayton was the one who made the final cut. With it, he alerted everyone, waking Remus. Dame walked to the bar, then began to force all of his weight against them. The damaged bar broke off, meaning we had enough room to fit things out of the cage.

Clayton took the bar, then did exactly what Dame did with the sword, only using the stubs of where the bar was broken as his beatstick. With a stronger material, we could get through the other bars significantly easier. Given all of us were awake, we watched as Remus used this new tool at an impressive speed. It took under an hour to get through the next bar. Clayton serrated this one too, so that he could join Remus's effort. Before long, we all were breaking bars off. Once we had a hole big enough for all of us to fit through, which was hard, given Dame was the size of an ox, we sat down and laughed. We had done it.

Chapter 39

From there, we needed to plan further. We could climb to the top of the cage from where we were, but that didn't do us much good. If we could get on top of the dragon, then kill the rider and take control, we could take it back to Parlania.

We brainstormed once again. I could use my blood abilities to hold sharpened bars to gouge holes into the dragon's armor and make it to the top, but my men couldn't. It seemed the dragon hijacking would be left up to me. I was in no fighting condition, as we were all malnourished. However, if I didn't act soon, my odds would only get worse and worse.

"I have an idea.", I spoke up, "I'm going to scale the dragon's armor using my tentacles holding the bars, then hopefully kill the dragon rider." Clayton asked, "Could you make the cuts at an angle? If so, we could shape these bars and follow you up." I hadn't thought of that. To make sure I could, I shaped rough dual hooks. I said, "Okay, but I want to test their strength first. I don't know if they'll carry you guys or not." Everyone nodded in agreement.

I climbed out of the cage, then hoisted myself to the top. Once I was at the top of the chain, I jammed my normal hooks into the dragon's thick armor. I hung from them with ease, meaning I could surely get on top. I then went back into the cage, grabbed two of the rougher crystal hooks, and tried to hang from the premade holes. To my surprise, they remained firm. I called for my men to come up to me. Only Remus and Clayton did. We all knew why Dame didn't come.

I continued to take chunks out of the dragon's armor and make my way to its side. Once I could use my feet to help me, I was able to scale it much easier. But just before I made it to the top, disaster struck.

I hear a snap, and then Remus yell in fear. I looked back to see one of his hooks falling to the ground below us. Remus shouted, "Son of a bitch! What do I do now?" Dame shouted, "Hold on, I'm going to make another and toss it to you!" Dame quickly went to work.
The hooks were made for both of them to hold weight, not only one. We heard the second snap.

Remus fell, screaming and flailing. Both Clayton and I yelled in fear along with him. Dame, thinking quickly, rushed to the hole we made in the cage. He grabbed Remus by his wrist, narrowly saving him. Remus puked all over his armor as he hung, earning him a cringeworthy expression mixed with relief on everyone's face. Once he was done, Dame pulled him up to the cage.

Remus thanked his savior, then threw up again, out of the side of the cage. We shook off what had just happened, then Clayton and I continued up the dragon.

Once I was up, I saw the rider. He was facing away from me, and fortunately couldn't hear us over the massive dragon's wings flapping.

I helped Clayton up, then readied my sword and shield. Clayton planned on using his hooks, which would hopefully be good at breaking the rider's armor off. Once the armor was off, I could effectively attack too. We stalked behind the rider, poised to jump.

CHAPTER 40

I nodded at Clayton to begin our assault. The rider was massive, about as big as Dame. It would've been fun to watch a fight between Dame with all of the sorrow in his heart and this behemoth.

Clayton smashed his crystal hooks into the riders shoulders, pulling him backwards, face up. I slammed my foot onto the rider's head over and over, wet crunches getting deeper with every step. Thinking we had already won, Clayton unearthed his hooks. I figured that the rider had to be dead after I just square danced on his face, but we were both mistaken.

The rider grabbed the hooks, yanked Clayton down onto him, then kicked him forward and nearly off the dragon. Clayton was lucky enough to slam both of his improvised weapons into the dragon's left eye, sliding down, tearing two massive wounds in the beast.

The dragon screeched in pain, then leaned heavily to its right. Clayton took this chance to easily climb his way back onto the dragon's head. The rider stood up, facing me. In a display of unique power, he stuck his hand up to the sky. Lightning struck him.

The heavy, spiked hammer from before materialized in his hands. Power surged between the cracks of his scales, illuminating the endless night sky. I put my sword and shield up, ready for a proper fight.

The rider swung his hammer over his head in a circle, then dropped it on me. I intercepted the blow with my shield, but was still knocked over. Once I was on the ground, the rider grabbed my ankle, attempting to brazenly throw me off. I swiped at his calf with my sword, but it clanked off. Before I could be thrown off, Clayton came to my rescue.

I saw the crystal hooks slide around the front of the dragonkin's knees, then plunge into them. Clayton pulled back, sending the rider forward. I was able to turn my leg and break out of his hold. Clayton then stood over the rider and drove his hooks into our opponent's shoulders, heaving his head up from the ground. Just as he was about to deliver the finishing blow, the dragon dove straight down.

Clayton and I slid backwards. I wedged my sword into a joint of the dragon's armor between its body and its wing. I stuck my arm out to Clayton, calling my shield back to save him. He grabbed on tightly, making sure he couldn't slip out of my grasp. The rider took a more unconventional approach, slamming the spikes of his weapon straight into the dragon's armor, and into its back. He hung from the maul's handle.

We heard Remus yell, "What the hell is going on up there?" There was so much wind being forced down my throat I couldn't attempt to talk. Once the dragon evened out, Remus yelled once more, "Hey! Is everything alright?" I yelled back, "No, not at all!" I was given no response.

Clayton let go and the rider got back up. I called my sword back, readying a shield in each hand. I couldn't damage the rider's armor at all, so I might as well avoid his strikes. The dragon let out a shrill screech, obviously in severe pain. The rider stood still, maul in hand, awaiting our approach. It was odd that he hadn't said anything. On the other hand, maybe there was nothing to say.

I charged at the rider, shields in front of me. He simply swiped me to the side with his maul, sending me stumbling. As he turned to hit me again, Clayton jumped on his back, grabbing the implanted hooks. He pulled one out, reached as far around the rider as he could, then slammed the hook into his gut.

The rider groaned, then leaned forward a little. I took advantage of this, throwing myself at him as hard as I could while he was off balance. My shoulder connected with the hook, driving it deeper. Clayton let go as I connected, getting out of the way of the falling giant.

I grabbed the deeply embedded hook, then pulled it across the rider's lower stomach, up into his chest. Green blood oozed from the crippling wound. I then tore the other hook from his shoulder and pried his armor apart. By the time that was done, the rider came back to reality.

He grabbed me around the throat, then stood up, hooks still inside of him. The rider then walked me to the edge of the dragon's body, ready to drop me. Clayton pulled back on the rider, hitting and screaming at him, to no avail.

Once the only thing under me was darkness, he let go. I dropped down, but was able to grab onto the dragon's wings before it was too late. I was almost thrown off with each powerful flap, but I refused to let go. The rider turned around and punched Clayton as hard as he could, sending him on his back.

In a desperate attempt, I did something stupid. I took my sword and slid it between hinges in the dragon's armor once more, sliding it across the dragon's wing. It howled in pain, then leaned to the left, just enough to make the rider lose his footing again. I wedged another sword into the next hinge up, cutting the dragon's wing into ribbons. It howled in pain every time, shifting and turning.

I got closer and closer to the dragon's back, mincing the webbing on its wings. Once I was close enough, I jumped back to the battleground. The rider was unaware of me, his focus set on Clayton. Before he had a chance to act, I sprinted behind him, grabbed each hook, pulled them out, then quickly plunged them back into his midsection. I then glided them across the same path I split his armor open with, opening his entire frontal cavity.

The rider dropped his hammer, and then to his knees. I let go of the hooks, then called upon my sword. He hung his head in defeat, exposing the back of his scaly neck for me to kill him. I had respect for this. Accepting defeat in battle was a rare trait from what I had heard, typically people continued to flail and fight. I lifted my sword, then ran it through the back of the rider's neck. I then kicked him off the edge, watching his body be swallowed by the empty, abyssal night.

We were now faced with a new issue. How the hell do we land a dragon?

Chapter 41

The dragon didn't have any reins to grab, or any kind of voice commands, to my knowledge. We were much too high up to jump or kill the dragon, and there wasn't anything to use to climb down.

The sun came over the horizon, turning all of the crystals blue once again. We were coasting just below the clouds, meaning we could see the plains below us. Trees sparsely populated the earthen floor, offering small variety in scenery.

Clayton and I took turns sitting exactly where the rider was, mimicking how he sat, seeing if that helped. As one would expect, nothing happened. Clayton then did what I thought would kill us all.

Clayton picked up his hooks and started to break through the dragon's head, chunks of bone and gobs of blood caking us. "What the hell are you doing?", I yelled in fear. He was going to kill us! The dragon spindled, trying to throw us off of his head. I heard Remus and Dame grunt as they slammed around the cage, luckily not falling out. I hung upside down using my swords, while Clayton crawled inside of the dragon's head, wedging himself between its brain and skull.

Once we evened back out, the dragon started to fly weaker and weaker, clearly dying. I heard Clayton yell, "Get ready son, we're depending on you!" I instantly shouted back, "What the fuck are you talking about? Get out of there, you idiot!" Clayton then tore into the dragon's brain, ripping and tearing it into pieces. Remus yelled from below, "Why are we falling? What did you dumbasses do?" The dragon nose dived, nearly throwing me off again. I kept my weapons embedded in the crystal as we dove towards the ground at impressive speed.

    Clayton yelled, "Those tentacles of yours boy, time to learn how to use them!" Was he fucking insane? Why is he gambling all of our lives on something I didn't even understand? Wind raged past my ears, which kind of hurt my eardrums. I panicked, trying to understand why Clayton would do this.

    Shouting once more, Clayton challenged, "Well, are we all going to die today, or are you going to get your shit together, son?" Trying to gather myself, I closed my eyes and focused on my bloodflow. My heart rate had been quickened, and not by my choice. Nothing was happening. The ground was getting closer, threatening to punch us. Remus screamed, "What the fuck did you do? You've killed us!" I strained myself, shaking from focusing so hard.

    Clayton reassured me, "You've got this, son! But I don't think any of us would mind you getting it sooner, rather than later!" I wasn't going to waste time by yelling back to him, instead planting my feet on the dragon's back, forcing myself to my limits. I could feel my blood bubble, boiling inside of me. It felt as though I was going to erupt into a ball of fire with how hot it was. I screamed as I felt my back break open, blood pouring down it, flowing to my legs and leaking from my under armor. "Keep going!", Clayton shouted. I heard Remus once again, but I couldn't make out what he was saying.

What felt like molten spears shot from my back, tearing the wounds open further. I started to cry from the pain. It hurt so bad that I was screaming loud enough for my lungs to feel like rupturing. The tentacles pierced through the dragon's armor, stabbing into its wings. I drew blood from the dragon itself, fueling myself with it. Dragon's blood was horrible, it gave me the same feeling as a handful of sand in one's mouth. Once I was in control of the dragon's wings, I pulled up on them.

I felt every limp shift in the beast's dead body, the weight of its armor, the fatigue in its muscles from flying for days on end. I felt bad for the dragon; it seemed it didn't want to carry prisoners around for its entire life. I guess it didn't matter what race you were, you would inevitably be ruled over by someone.

Clayton cheered, "I knew you could do it, boy! Keep going!" Remus and Dame quit shouting in fear, now laughing. Remus insulted, yet congratulated me, "You're doing it! This is probably the worst thing I've ever been a part of, along with being the stupidest chance I've ever seen taken, but I'll be damned!"

I continued to push and pull on the dragon's wings, leveling us out. The pain didn't die down, but I became accustomed to it, only grunting and yelping in discomfort. Once we were stable in the air, I began our descent. I don't know how the hell I was doing this, but I was. Just because I had done it didn't mean I thought Clayton was any less crazy, his idea was still dangerously unhinged.

Once we touched down, which was a rather rough landing, we all took a second to laugh in relief. My tentacles slurped back inside of me, closing my back. The dragon was completely dry of blood, meaning I had chosen a good time to land. Clayton crawled out of the cracked skull, coated in meaty chunks and blood. Dame and Remus fumbled their ways nauseously out of the cage, which was on its side, and ran out to help us get down to the ground.

We all laid down in the knee high grass, enjoying being grounded again. Dame joked, "If I so much as jump, I think I'll puke. I don't ever want to leave the ground again." We all chuckled in agreement. The group agreed we should take a well-earned nap, as we were all beyond exhausted.

I had done it. My brothers and I lived to fight another day.

Chapter 42

Once we were all awake, we had to plan on how to get back to civilization. Clayton said he recognized this land from a previous war. I had wondered how many people he had killed, being as old and knowledgeable in combat as he was. He mentioned fighting in multiple wars, meaning his head count had to be impressive.

Taking a crack at trying to get him to open up about his past, I asked Clayton, "How do you recognize this area? If you know it, can you get us back home?" He stood up, pulled some strains of grass, and replied, "This is switchgrass and indiangrass, which means we should be between Parlania and Talithia. With the lack of trees, we can't be near Talithia, meaning we're closer to Parlania. If I was to guess, I'd say we're maybe 20 kilometers from home. We flew North for what, two days? That was after walking South for five or six days, which means we surely flew farther North than we walked South. If we walk South starting now, we should be able to get home by midnight, given the terrain stays the same."

We all groaned, as our flasks, and stomachs, were empty. If Panther wasn't a spy, he could've hunted down something for us to eat. Clayton compromised, "Alas, maybe we should stay put for the night. Remus, Dame, if you two wouldn't mind ripping out a large perimeter of grass, maybe we could start a fire. Make sure that you tear everything out of the ground, stomp it down, and make the area large, we don't want to get stuck in a grass fire. I'm going to scrounge around for any food, sometimes elderberries will grow in these conditions." Clayton looked at me and continued, "And you, you aren't done yet. I'm going to teach you how to hunt." While I wanted nothing more than to hibernate until I was Clayton's age, he was right, I should learn. As he's shown us, he clearly has a lot to teach.

*   *   *

Clayton started by breaking off a decent sized branch from a tree by having me hang off of it and shimmy. Once it came loose, I fell to the ground. Clayton laughed, then helped me up. He then instructed me to shovel mud, using my hands, onto a big rock. I didn't see the point in this, but I listened. Once the entire rock was caked, Clayton told me to wipe all of it off. "What was the point in this if I'm just going to take it off?" If I'm being honest, I was a little upset that he had wasted our time.

Clayton replied, "I trusted you, now it's your turn to trust me." I reluctantly agreed, scooping handfuls of mud back to the ground.

Clayton pointed out, "Okay, now the rock is wet, yes? The moisture in the mud did that. Now, I want you to run the broken end of that branch against the rock, preferably on a jagged edge. Do this until you feel it's sharp enough. If you need to rewet it, you know where the mud is." Clayton then walked away. "Where are you going?", I asked. Without turning around, he answered, "My portion of work. Don't worry, I'll be back."

    Alone, I scraped the branch against the wet boulder, very slowly shaping and breaking pieces off. Once the actual tip shape was made, which took what seemed like forever, the process was made significantly easier. I only had to reapply mud once, and noticed it had lost most of its moisture for the second application. Once I was done, I stuck the unsharpened end against a rock, then stomped on it, shortening it to a more manageable length.

    Clayton came back about half an hour later, while I sat in the grass, waiting. His helmet was full of small, blackish purple berries. He informed me that they were elderberries, and could grow in the plains next to wet patches. "Well, I'm going to drop these off at camp, and then we can go kill something to eat, yeah?" I nodded in agreement.

    Once we got back to the camp, we saw that Dame and Remus had made good progress. A massive pile of grass sat in the middle of a ring that was around 12 feet wide. Clayton told them they were doing good, but had to keep going to prevent a wildfire. Clayton set the berries down. He said, "Now I know these are enticing, but don't put them anywhere near your mouth, unless you want a river to run out of both ends of you." Dame asked, "Then why the hell did you nab them?" Clayton responded,

"You'll see, have faith" We then turned away, leaving to find ourselves a meal.

Chapter 43

Clayton and I laid in the grass, then covered ourselves with it. I was sweating, as the sun shone on the grass, heating it on my back. I was able to slow my heart rate enough to where I wasn't miserable, but it was still toasty. We sat right on the edge of what Clayton said was undoubtedly boar feeding grounds. Something to do with certain figs growing here, a few looking like they had been nibbled on, and that there was a small pond nearby.

We sat still for close to an hour before we heard grass shifting behind us. Clayton looked at me, silently saying that we might have something here. Footsteps crunched past us, making its way up our left side. I kept completely still, breathing as shallowly as I could. My makeshift spear was in my right hand, sitting between Clayton and I.

Now that I took a minute to ponder, why didn't I just use my sword, rather than this shoddy spear? I suppose it had something to do with teaching me a lesson. Besides, if Clayton was kind enough to teach me a few things, I was more than willing to learn.

After a few minutes passed, 3 boars came into sight. The smallest one was closest to me, and within reach. Clayton knew I was about to stab the pig, but grabbed my spear, staring me down. The biggest one was well out of reach, I don't know why he wanted me to wait.

The boars ate, and a few more came out. We almost had one step right on us, but it walked the opposite direction just before it did. There were a handful of them now, but none in reach. I don't know why Clayton didn't just let me poke the porky bastard, but I figured his judgment was better than mine.

We watched our prey for close to 40 minutes until the biggest one came into our range. He stood facing us. Clayton slightly nodded at me to strike.

Following orders, I rammed the spear into the boar's chest, puncturing him deeply. It hellishly squealed, then turned around and ran. I jumped up, which Clayton followed. My mentor proudly said, "Hey! Damn good job son!" I'm not sure what he meant; all of the boars ran off as fast as they could, including the one I struck. Noticing my disappointed expression, Clayton told me, "Don't worry, you hit him good. He won't be running very far. Follow the blood, I'll follow you."

Doing as I was told once more, I followed the blood. It was made easy, as I could sense it. As we got closer to the animal, I could feel its fear. Its heart was beating fast, and it was losing a lot of blood. I told myself not to absorb any until I found him, that way the trail didn't disappear. We walked for about five minutes before finding the boar. It was laying down, shallowly breathing. Clayton ordered me, "Kill it swiftly, son. No need for it to suffer more than needed." I jammed my spear into the boar's head, killing it.

Clayton put his arm around me and on my shoulder, congratulating me, "That was a damn good job, son. Damn good job." I had never been told I was doing a good job before. I wasn't sure how to take this new emotion. What I can say is that having someone be proud of you is one of the best feelings in the world.

Clayton took twine he made from grass and reeds, tied it around the pigs front and back feet, then to my spear. He lifted one side on his shoulder, and I did the same with the other. We hauled the boar back to camp, ready to eat again.

That walk back was a magical one. I felt nothing short of accomplished. I felt like I was enough. I hadn't grappled with the thought that I was never enough for anyone before, I just figured that was how life was. I was glad, no, blessed, to have met Clayton.

Chapter 44

I was met with applause and wide eyes once we returned, which reinforced the pride I already had in my heart further. Once we sat the pig down, Clayton told the others to start a fire. Remus left to gather branches and the like, while Dame continued to expand our circle.

Clayton walked me through how to gut the pig, and allowed me to use my powers to create a knife. I also used my power to bleed the boar out instantly. Clayton informed me I wouldn't have this convenience next time we hunted, but I had learned enough for the day. I was extremely grateful for all that he had taught me. Not only because it benefited all of us as a group, but because it was out of the kindness of his heart.

Once I finished cutting up the boar, Remus got ready to make a spit. We had a small fire going. Before Remus could get too far, I had an idea.

I sat down facing the fire while Clayton held onto the raw meat. I focused once again, trying to control my tentacles. Now that I had a conscious idea of what I had to do, maybe it would come easier. Although my eyes were closed, I knew everyone was watching me closely. A sharp pain split my shoulder blade open, and a blood tentacle left. I guided it towards the meat, stabbing it. I then brought it over the fire, turning it. Everyone smiled in approval.

Remus asked, "Okay, but what about these berries?" Clayton responded, "Ah, that's right. I'm going to need everyone's helmets." Listening, we all forked over our helmets. Clayton waved Dame over, then had him distribute the berries across each helmet, then crush them with his big meaty hands. Just as he was about to take a sip, Clayton swatted at his hand and said, "Hey, no. They'll still make you shit a flood. Have to boil the toxins out." He looked over to me as he said the last part.

Rather than opening my back once more, I branched out the tentacle I already had, cradling the helmets. I then brought them over the fire as well. We all sat down next to the bonfire, waiting for the food to finish.

*   *   *

Once Clayton deemed the berries to be good enough, I took them off of the flame. Dame dug up some cold mud, and I put the helmets inside of it. The meat took longer, however, it finished about the same time as the elderberry juice cooled.

We feasted on unseasoned, gamey boar and tart, warm elderberry juice. It was horrible. It was amazing. How it managed to be both at once, I couldn't put into words. We drank from our own helmets, which left a salty, coin-like flavor on the lips. We used our breast plates as a normal plate, chewing off of large slabs of meat.

Once we were full, we laid down on piles of grass. It was kind of funny, Dame probably used more grass than all of us combined. I stared into the sky, star gazing. I had always wondered how people saw constellations, it all just looked like dots to me. I guess one can find anything if they really look hard enough. I felt myself slowly drifting off into slumber, ready for my well earned rest.

Chapter 45

    I awoke once the chalice that held the sun spilt its warmth onto my face. Covering my eyes with my hands, the light hurt me at first. After slowly sitting up, I stretched my legs. It didn't occur to me until now, but I was incredibly sore from all of the recent battling.

    I saw that Clayton had woken up before me, and he was sitting next to the smoldering embers of our dying fire. Dame was laying on his back, snoring like the bull he was. Remus tried to cover himself in grass to keep warm in his sleep, but it all fell at his sides, presumably due to rolling around.

    Once everyone was awake, we trusted Clayton to take us back to Parlania. He told us it would be roughly a six hour walk if we didn't stop for breaks.

* * *

    It didn't take long for us to get out of the grasslands, as there wasn't any thick foliage to stop us. Occasionally some grass would wrap around your boot and you'd stumble, but that was about it. The woods, however, offered a much greater challenge.

    Within minutes Remus stepped on a trigger for a net trap, which pulled him into a tree. He yelped as he went up, wildly discombobulated. Alert, we all readied ourselves for a fight. When one ceased to arrive, Dame tore the rope in half with his hand, slowly letting Remus down.

    Clayton warned, "Ah, I was hoping it wasn't true." I inquired, "Hope what wasn't true? There's clearly something I'm missing here." He answered, "Well, quite frankly, the Talithians think us Parlanians to be a sort of sickness spreading across the land. I feared they would've set up traps to stop us from invading after Scaf's murder, but remained hopeful." Remus snobbishly corrected, "Remained naive, you mean." Being the bigger man, Clayton ignored him and continued to lead us through the wilderness.

    After a few more close calls with a handful of creative traps, we had made our way to the woodline to another grassy field. Clayton nodded his head, thinking out loud, "Okay, I know for sure where we are now." Remus asked, "Well, how do you know that?" Clayton replied, "I speared my first deer around these grasslands. I could show you exactly where it happened if you'd like" Everyone groaned in disapproval, as we all yearned for home. Taking the hint, we were led the original route.

    It was just before noon when we saw billowing black smoke climbing into the sky. Clayton picked up his pace. While no one said it, I knew that it was coming from Parlania. Were we under attack? My legs felt like they could've given out at any moment, my muscles aching terribly. I had no choice but to fight through it.

As we got closer and closer, we heard the familiar sound of battle. The screaming of women and children in fear, and of men in agony. Crackling fire, and clanging from weapons colliding.

There was another small section of woods, no longer than 300 feet, that separated us from Parlania. Just as we broke out of the other side of the woods, I saw exactly what I feared.

Dragonkin soldiers hacked away at unarmed peasants and royal guards alike, their thick armor hardly even chipping at the strikes of our steel. Familiar hovels and storefronts were either encased in an inferno, or had collapsed into a pile of smoldering embers. The sun sat in the middle of the sky, although I'm not sure we needed it to see what was happening, given the ferocious blaze.

Parlania, my corrupted home, was under invasion. Part of me wanted to leave it to burn, leveling into ashes. I'm not sure why, but I forced that thought out, mentally ridiculing myself. We charged, ready to defend our brethren.

CHAPTER 46

Everyone other than me was completely unarmed, which meant my brothers would be picking up the fallen's cutlery. A slit opened in my wrists, my weapons leaking out and forming in hand.

We turned the corner around a burning building, its smoke momentarily blocking my vision. Once we were in the street, the only thing to see was carnage. Gutted wives laying next to their either crying or equally slain children, with minced soldiers littered around. The only thing that was unique about this slaughter was that it wasn't our doing; it was done unto us.

I had to get to the palace and make sure Parla was alive. If he was dead, he couldn't reverse what he had done to my brother. Everyone nabbed bloodied weapons from the ground, hoping they'd serve them better than their previous owner. As my crew and I made our way down the wet dirt streets, stepped over and around the dead, we ran into a small dragonkind cleanup crew. They were armed with the normal crystalline armor and lightning greatswords.

Not taking any time to prepare, Remus charged in with a shortsword, followed by the rest of us. Before the dragonkind could ready for battle, we cut them to pieces. Not focused on anyone else's fight, I slid my sword under a plate in a dragonkind's armor, right into his lower spine.

With a short breath, he dropped dead. Once the patrol had been felled, we continued toward the palace.

    I glanced past a bar Dad used to gamble at, watching embers consume it. Good riddance. The streets turned into arranged cobbles, the sounds of warfare leaking into my ears, getting louder and louder the further we ran. We turned the final corner to the palace, finding the source of the noise.

    Parlanian warriors were scattered around, both as corpses and duelists. They fought the dragonkin to the best of their ability, but couldn't match the strength of the sky reptiles. Without hesitation, my men charged, minimally armed and exhausted. The courage that irradiated from them was contagious, capable of inspiring even the most pitiful men.

    I charged behind a rather mediocre dragonkin, resting my angled palm on his back so that my sword could form inside of him, penetrating his thick hide. But, I was too late; the soldier he was fighting lay on the ground, a grievous ax splintering his shoulder open, convulsing from electric shock, leaving his gore to ooze out into the streets.

    A dragon knight came at me from my left side, trying to make me a kebab with a lengthy, pointed spear. I smacked his weapon away with my shield, leaving his torso wide open. Before I could deliver a fatal blow, I heard another dragon's heavy footsteps behind me.

    Continuing my arm's motion, I kept swinging my shield back, hitting the dragon on the side of their head.

The first dragon regathered himself as I stabbed my crimson blade diagonally into the other's collarbone, the tip exiting his ribs opposite of my hilt. The lightning spear-wielding dragon swiped his spear at the back of my neck, which I ducked, and then jabbed at my midsection. I moved slightly to the side, able to turn an impalement into a graze. I felt my meat slide apart, opening itself into the surrounding ashen air.

    I called my sword back and grabbed their weapon just below its point while it was extended, using my shield to break it in half. Fighting through the electricity coursing through me, with a quick movement, I used the business end to slash at the dragon. He blocked my first attack using the spear's handle, but it broke in half. I lunged forward once more, trying to stick the bastard. He bumped backs with Dame, who threw himself backwards into the dragon, sending him forward on to his own weapon.

    With our presence, the dragon's chances at victory slimmed greatly. I ran up the stairs to the palace, swiping at a dragon's ankles who was ahead of me. He fell forward, roaring in pain. I ran past him, having no time to spare. He would die slowly in agony from blood loss, but I had to assure Devon's safety. Perhaps if he was lucky, someone would finish him off, or he'd do it himself.

    The doors were already open, bodies spread here, just like everywhere else. Oddly, Parla sat in his throne, wearing the same grin he always did. His toga was drenched in blood, but none of it his own. Standing a few feet from his throne was Helena, equally unscathed. She cast a glare back at me, first confused, then impressed. Helena complimented, "Some son you've raised here, Parla." It felt as if every organ inside of me shut down in dread, becoming a muddled mess. Son?

CHAPTER 47

All I could do was stand, my mind in disarray. Son? What was she talking about? Helena continued, turning back to Parla, "You haven't even told him yet, have you?" Parla's smug expression turned serious as he sat forward, insulting, "You always were a meddling bitch, mother." Helena turned back to me again, taking a twisted pity on me, "You poor child. You've been born to kill and die, exactly like the rest, but so uniquely. I'm sorry for what will inevitably befall you."

Snapping out of my trance, I shakily yell, "What the hell are you talking about? Son? That can't be right, I watched my parents die!" Parla wiped his hand down his beard, opening his mouth. Before he could get anything out, I interrupted in a flurry of rage, "No more of your games! Tell me the truth!" Parla stood, looking down at me with a sinister gaze, warning, "You're disrespect is justified, but disrespect regardless. Watch your tone, boy." Ignoring him, I challenged, "Come and do something about it."

Helena laughed, poking fun at Parla, "Seems you've a defiant one. Maybe he wasn't raised properly?" Parla raised his voice slightly, agitated by his threatened authority, "You have no place to speak, you sickening mutant." Helena pursed her lips, taking the degradation. Feeling ignored and jested, I demanded once more, "What is she talking about?"

Parla slowly paced towards me, saying in the most demeaning tone, "Fine, boy. You're a God. Is that what you want to hear? The second you slid out of your whore of a mother's legs I offered a poor beggar family a large sum of money to get you out of my sight. Your piece of shit false father was a gambler, and I knew this. I also knew of their other son's sickness, and that bitch of a mother. I knew they'd run you into the ground, leaving only desperation and anger brewing inside of you. They bred you to be my ultimate soldier without even knowing it. Do you think it's a coincidence my priestesses knew exactly where to find you when I needed you? Us having the same powers? How about that scummy gangster you called Chubby? He was a paid actor, just like your guardians. Once they fulfilled their usage, I had you all kill each other. That boy in the other room, erm, Devon was it? I didn't even give him that sickness, he was merely unlucky. Well, lucky for me I suppose, but that's besides the point. You are a God, Dylan, and I made you for one purpose. To make me King of the Gods."

I felt myself shatter. I couldn't think. I couldn't feel. All I could do was repeat those final words in my head over and over, *"You are a God, Devon, and I made you for one purpose. To make me the King of the Gods."* My weapons slowly crept back inside as I slumped to the ground, kneeling to my true father. I asked monotonically, "My mother, who was she?"

Helena scoffed, "Oh, just some barn slut he decided he needed on one of his meaningless raids. Don't you see, child? He's using you. You can't allow that. Please, come with me." Parla sat down calmly once again, clearly stating, "Leave and I kill them. I know that friendship you soldiers make, it'd be tragic if something was to ail them. Or even better, maybe a humiliating public execution for desertion! I could blame them for leaving The House of Scaf, letting their comrades die so they will only live on in infamy. But that's up to you, of course."

Helena walked towards me lifting my head, her hand on my chin. While I expected reassurance, I was met with further demoralization. "Do what he says, child. You've seen what he does to those that don't. Care for those around you while you can, even if it means bowing to someone like him." She walked out, leaving me alone.

CHAPTER 48

I laid on my bed as a priest stitched my side shut. I reveled in the feeling of the needle piercing and stretching my flesh back together. The pain felt incredible, but it couldn't help take my mind off of what just unfolded. Not only had I been born to be used, I was lied to three separate times about who I was. First, I was a poor peasant. Then, I was a God's chosen warrior to save my country. Finally, realistically, I am a toy for some warlord that turns out to be my father.

I slept on and off for days, eating like a hunting hound and bathing like a diva as my exterior wounds healed. I'm not sure any amount of wine could drown my thoughts, nor could any soapy water wash my guilt away. I came to the disgusting conclusion that for the good of my men and their legacy, I had to keep working as Parla's harbinger of destruction. My crew could never know. What would they think of me?

As the sun set on another night. It had been about a week since Parla broke the news to me. Sometimes I did nothing but sleep out of fatigue, but others I couldn't fall asleep, no matter how badly I wanted to, thanks to the demons whispering in my head. A few times I told myself I could simply kill Parla, but I quickly got rid of those, as that was implausible. I might be a God, and I might be strong, but I'll never be what he is. Maybe that wasn't a bad thing.

* * *

A slight knock landed on my door, the sound creeping under and into my ears. I groaned, not wanting to get up. The door opened, meaning whoever it was wasn't a priest or priestess; they wouldn't enter unless told. Clayton stepped through the doorway, glancing around my room. He chuckled, "The things I would've done for all of this at your age. You'd ought to feel lucky." Clayton sat in a chair in the corner of the room. He prodded, "Have to get up sometime, y'know. C'mon, Dame has been asking about you nonstop, if you do-" I cut Clayton off, "Alright, alright, I'll be out in a bit. Although your ugly mug is no way to start my day", I grinned as I said. Clayton stood up, pointed at me, and jokingly fired back, "Careful, or I'll leave you uglier than me, son"

Before Clayton stepped out, he turned and reminded me, "You know, you're the youngest of us, you should probably be the fir-" I threw my pillow at Clayton's head, motioning that I got the message. I could hear a hearty laugh from the other side of the door.

With a large sigh and lackluster motivation, I rolled out of bed. Mimicking every other day, after a long bath and divine breakfast, I stepped into the throne room. Just before I was about to leave, an unwelcome voice called out to me, "I paid for the best inn for them. While they're our servants, they deserve some comfort." Without looking back at Parla, I coldly stated, "They aren't my servants." Parla snickered, knowing he had struck a nerve.

People moved around me on the street as I made my way to the Red Inn. All of Parla's important playthings stayed at the Red Inn, giving the illusion of importance and respect on his behalf. The complete opposite of normal inns, this one was rather clean and quiet. Red carpets and cushions combined with lightly polished oak wood made for extravagant furniture and a welcoming aesthetic. Large oil lamps hung around the ceiling, offering a dim, yet cozy atmosphere. There was a single man sitting next to a cobbled fireplace that was surrounded by chairs and sofas, otherwise, there wasn't anybody in sight.

I stopped at the bar, looking around behind the desk for any service. When none came, I turned back to glance at the man sitting next to the fireplace. He was gone now too. Being alone in such a profligate environment felt kind of eerie. Luckily, it didn't last long, for the bartender came out from a small door, probably leading to a storage room.

She was a rather plain girl, sporting long blonde hair and a tight, red dress. While she wasn't anything special on the eyes, she didn't lack either. A rather soft, yet confident voice perked up, "Oh! You should've called for me, I'm sorry! How can I help you?" Paying no attention to the apology, I asked, "Looking for my crew. One of them is down a leg, one looks like he could wrestle a bear with a single hand, another old enough to remember the past generation of God's, and the other a brazen warrior." After biting her lip and thinking for a bit, the bartender looked back at me, "If they're who I'm thinking of, they headed out to meet up with a friend over at The Steak Garden.

The Steak Garden is exactly what it sounds like. They had weird paintings of chicken legs growing out of flower stems, and other absurd things. While odd, it had its own fun and unique gimmick. I dug in my toga pocket for a coin, setting it on the bar as I made my way out. The bartender, seemingly used to minimal closure on conversations, didn't say anything else. Following the trail of breadcrumbs, I set out for The Steak Garden.

Chapter 49

A short iron fence surrounded a kindly pavilion, housing tables full of hungry customers. On the outside, lush shrubbery made for a rather natural feeling. The smell of freshly braised beef grew stronger as I neared the entrance, along with the sounds of clinking cutlery and waitresses hurriedly delivering food.

I passed through the mock gate, already opened and only there for design, and was met with a bright smile from a rather distinguished gentleman. He had silver hair, and a respectable, well kept beard. His tidy suit resembled the prestige of the restaurant, as silly as the theme of it was.

"Welcome to The Steak Garden, sir, how may I help you?", he asked in a reserved, yet positive way. I responded, "I'm here to meet a few friends. Soldiers, they are most likely obnoxiously burping, one is down a leg?" The waiter instantly knew who I was talking about, and with a slight drop in his mood, he waved for me to follow him, "This way, sir."

Following the man, I bobbed around tables, most being full of upper-class families and high-ranking soldiers. It seemed to be a busy day, especially for an attack happening not so long ago. Not before long, I heard one of Dame's instantly recognizable booming belches, followed by loud laughter.

"Here you are, sir. Is there anything I might get for you?", the waiter asked, hiding his annoyance. I sat down at the table, nodding in acknowledgment to my men while telling the man that I didn't want anything. Handing the server a coin, he took a graceful bow and left, wishing us all well.

I exchanged greetings with everyone, noticing their bubbly happiness. That is, everyone but Izac. Izac offered nothing to me but a solemn nod, clearly still grappling with the loss of his leg. I sincerely hoped he'd cheer up soon, as unlikely as it was. They were already done with their meals, now only drinking premium bourbon and burping loudly. Izac was clearly only drinking to be drunk, but he was contributing to the high bill no less.

Clayton invited me to the conversation, taunting, "I was wondering how long it was going to take you. We waited for what felt like forever, but ended up eating without you. For having the power of a God, you sure are slow." I shot back, "Careful, or I'll beat you until your meal ends up in your pants." After a good laugh, I got a mug of bourbon myself. Not downing it like the other pigs at the table, I tried to enjoy it. I was still sore, no point in partying too hard yet. Remus asked, "Well?" I was met with interested eyes, as if I was supposed to know exactly what that one word question meant. I looked back confused, to which Dame prodded, "You aren't drunk yet, don't pretend to be dazed and confused, what did Parla say?"

I bit my tongue. I wanted to tell them about my Godhood, I really did, but I couldn't. What would it do to our relationship? They'd all treat me differently.

I answered, "Well, all I know is that we're safe from invasion for a while. I don't think that dragonkin will be coming back. Helena said something about us starting a war with killing her son, but I find that to be unlikely. Now that Scaf is dead, we can finally be at some kind of peace. I think the Gods are finally done killing each other."

Izac scoffed, adding, "Yeah, right." I glanced over at him inquisitively, "What do you mean by that?" "Nevermind", he brashly concluded. We all sat in an uncomfortable silence for a little while. However, it ended when Remus let loose a burp sounding similar to a lion's growl. A few dirty looks were shot over at us, but we didn't care.

Once everyone other than me was sloppily drunk, we decided it was time to head back to the inn for the night. The bill was handed to Clayton, which he studied closely. He set the bill face-down, beckoning, "Well, I say we leave Remus to wash the dishes, and bolt, yeah?" We all jokingly stood up quickly, excluding Izac, to which Remus yelled for us to wait. After a hearty laugh, we divided up the bill and left. Dame carried Izac on his back. I could sense a sort of tension between them. Dame's regret and Izac's bitterness made for an unusual dynamic between the two of them.

Patrons and staff alike angrily watched us depart, dually glad we were leaving. I had to guide my crew down the street, trying to keep everyone upright. In one especially near-miss, Dame almost fell backwards onto Izac. I luckily got behind and leaned into him, likely saving Izac's life.

Once we got back inside the Red Inn, Clayton had to lead us to their room. He walked all over every side of the hall, fumbling around like a toddler that had just learned how to walk. Eventually, after everyone fought over what the room number was, we found ourselves inside of a rather luxurious room.

Keeping the same theme, red carpet and fabric made up most of the furniture, along with the pleasantly polished oak. There were 4 beds, one for each of them. I bid them all goodnight, before leaving them to their own devices. I left the Red Inn much quieter than I came in.

When drunken fools weren't wandering the halls, it was rather quiet, the only sound being the innkeeper from before putting chairs up on the table. Before I could leave, she caught my attention, "Excuse me?" I turned around, notioning I was listening, "I know what you all did. I want to thank you, for protecting us against Scaf and Helena." I nodded, accepting the thanks, and went to turn once more, only for her to continue, "Be honest with me. Is it over?"

I faced her, making eye contact and answering, "I do not know."

Chapter 50

Rather than sleeping in for hours on end like previous days, I woke up before the sun had even completely risen. I completed my typical routine, returning to my room, feeling fresh and ready to tackle the day. Knowing my brothers would still be sleeping and hungover, I made my way out to the throne room. The plan was to wander around town today, doing some random shopping, and just enjoy myself overall. Seeing everyone yesterday lifted my mood, even if it hurt to see Izac so glum.

Just before I was able to leave, Parla called out, "Back to your typical schedule. Everything went well yesterday, I presume?" I coldly replied, "Yes.", trying to hurry out. Parla interrupted my departure once more, "Ah, wait. I have something for you." Taking the hint, I turned around, and walked to the base of the steps to Parla's throne. Parla stood, motioning for me to come closer.

Following orders, I came to the foot of the throne. It seemed a little smaller up close, but was still impressively decadent. "Sit.", Parla commanded. I looked at him dumbfounded, confused as to why he wanted me to sit on his throne. He repeated, "Go ahead, sit on the throne, boy." My stomach churned as I slowly sat down in the throne. It was rather uncomfortable, not fitting my size whatsoever. I looked up at Parla, wondering what he was getting at.

He continued, "This is going to be yours someday. I know you don't understand it now, but it will be. How does it feel?" I answered honestly, "It feels pointless. A throne isn't the mark of a good ruler, that is given by one's ability to lead proficiently." Parla chuckled, "So, you've returned a philosopher. Again, you'll understand soon enough. I wanted to give something to you before I give you your next task." The God of Wrath and Blood held his hand out to me, offering for me to take it. Standing up, I shook his hand. Parla used his nail to peel part of my hand open, drawing blood. I was taken back to a familiar place.

A thin layer of blood coated the floor in every direction, being the only thing in sight, not counting the clear sky overhead. This was similar to where Parla and I first met and he gave me my powers. I looked around, seeming to be alone.

A voice called behind me, "I'm over here" I turned, facing Parla's blood red apparition. I asked, "Why are we here again?" Parla stated blankly, "I'm going to teach you how to control it." Not sure what he meant, I felt my heart rate increasing slightly.

"I want you to focus on your breathing. Let your heart beat hard, it should feel like a drum in your chest.", Parla commanded. Listening, I closed my eyes, forcing deep, long breaths. My heart started to beat faster. Parla stopped me, "No, not faster. I want it to beat harder. Make your breaths more exaggerated and spaced, not quick, like you're running a mile." Listening, I started to exhale loudly, holding my breath for about half of a second before starting my next. My heart slowed down, starting to thump deeper and deeper.

"Good, now maintain that.", Parla ordered. Suddenly, something hard struck me in the nose, causing me to lose my focus and open my eyes. I went to ask what happened, but was stopped by Parla, "You can't fight with your eyes closed, boy. Try again, but do it as you would in a fight." Hesitantly, I followed his orders.

Once I had gotten back on track, Parla picked up a handful of blood from the ground, then threw it at me once more. I ducked it, keeping my breathing correct. Parla laughed, "You already know how to evade attacks, boy. Stand still, let your blood protect you." I then realized he was trying to teach me how to use my tentacles.

Another ball of blood flew my way. I felt my back split slowly, but I was hit before I could do anything. "Again.", Parla ordered, throwing another. No matter how many times I got hit, I couldn't seem to do it fast enough. With every failure, Parla raised his tone more. Another ball hit my chest, the tentacle hardly wrapping over my shoulder this time. "Again!", Parla yelled. I was starting to get angry; his tone and being hit upset me.

After a few more attempts, Parla was screaming, picking up the pace at which he threw projectiles at me. No matter what, I couldn't seem to be fast enough. With the next hitting my nose once more, Parla barked, "Again!", to which I yelled back, "What do you want from me?" Parla shot forward to me at the speed of light, hoisting me up by the throat, stopping my breathing and ruining my heart rate.

He yelled, "I want you to kill for me, dammit! You're a weak, emotional child, incapable of even the most menial tasks! Yo-" I exploded in a rage, three tentacles forming from my back. One wrapped around Parla's waist, squeezing him tightly, the other two grabbing his upper and lower arm, pulling in different directions to break his elbow. Parla dropped me, showing my success. His arm swiftly healed, to which he snickered, "There it is, that anger I'm all too familiar with. Use it. Again." Another blood ball flew at me, to which I intercepted with a tentacle.

Giving me no time to celebrate, Parla casted another my way, then another. Soon, he was throwing a monsoon of things my way, all of different shapes, sizes, and speeds. My tentacles countered them all, not allowing a single one to hit me. Parla laughed, "Yes! Yes, there it is! You are a killer, aren't you? A ruthless killing machine, only good for your anger! Keep going!"

His words pissed me off further. Every time my heart beated it felt like a cannon being shot inside of my chest. My breathing was instinctual now, not forced. With a final, massive projectile, the sun was blocked out. This ball had to have been as big as a sizable townhouse, flying at an impressive speed.

I dug my feet into the ground, intercepting the ball with multiple tentacles. It pushed me back, creating ripples in the water, but I refused to let it hit me. I screamed as I fought back, giving this challenge everything I had. It neared me, and I could feel myself slipping. Parla chirped up, "Go ahead, show me what a real ruler is, since you know so much about it. Show me your power, boy!" His voice agitated me, giving me the strength to better fight back.

I pivoted my foot, using my tentacles to toss the massive ball like a shot-put. Parla excitedly laughed once more, "There it is!" I dropped to my knees, exhausted. My breathing slowly calmed back down, allowing me to regain my mentality again. Parla walked over to me, and offered his hand to help me up. Once our hands connected, I was sent back into the real world once more.

Parla moved me out of the way with a smirk, sitting back in his throne. "A basic skill, that was. Don't consider me impressed, but yourself lucky that I haven't pushed you too hard yet." I limply made my way down the stairs, not sure what to feel. Parla called out once more, "Be grateful, boy. It's a gift for your victory against Scaf, but also training for your next campaign. However, you aren't ready for that now. Go clean yourself up, gather your troops, and meet back here in a timely manner."

I could only listen to him, and do his bidding. Slinking back to my room, I gathered myself once more.

Chapter 51

We stood in front of Parla, all asking in unison, "You want us to do what?" Parla smugly repeated himself, "Talithia. I want it." My crew and I were baffled. We had just defended ourselves against Scaf and taken his city, why were we now turning our attention to Talithia? I spoke up, "We're at peace, why in the hell would we do that?" Parla snickered, "Ah, you don't understand war, boy. Here's how it works: Scaf attacked us, so we victoriously retaliated. That much is true. However, in doing so, we've proven we can not only defend against two separate invasions, but also storm and kill a God. That strikes fear into the hearts of the other Gods. With them afraid of us, they'll inevitably attack. We must act first to save time and troops."

None of my men said anything, for if they spoke up, they'd be hung for defying a God. However, this was something I could get away with. I continued, "And how do you know they'll attack us? If they're so afraid, I would think they'd hide away and avoid us, no?" Parla countered, "Boy. When an animal is scared, what does it do? It lashes out to defend itself, even if not in any immediate danger. We need to get ahead of this."

Before I could speak up again, General Starfli entered the room. She took a knee, along with my men. Without any respect for the piece of shit, I stood defiantly. Parla remarked, "Ah, good, General Starfli. I was just informing your new polemarches and fellow general of our plans. I trust my informant told you the plan?" Starfli nodded, paying no mind to the rest of us. I asked her, "How can you go along with this?" Starfli answered, "Because it's my duty. It'd serve you well to learn yours." I was furious. This is why he taught me to better control my power, he wanted me to use it to slaughter an undeserving community.

Parla finished, "Train well, gather new recruits, you march a month from now. Oh, and one more thing. Dame, Izac, I have something for you." A priest stepped forward, carrying a sturdy basket with a package inside. Dame set Izac down, opening the gifts on the ground together. Izac pulled out a quiver and shortbow, while Dame unwrapped thick dual greatswords. "I know how much he means to you, might as well take him along." Dame put the basket on his back and picked Izac up, setting him inside.

Izac spoke up, which has been a rarity lately, "It's comfortable, and the bow is well sized for me. I've never shot a bow before, but I'll learn if it means I get to come with. Thank you, Lord." Dame wrapped his swords back up, thanking Parla as well. Parla demanded of the priests, "Give them theirs too, hurry. They don't have all day, unlike you bums." Clayton was given a rather impressive glaive, its blade slightly curved and extremely fine looking. Remus was given a new broadsword and buckler shield, which he needed. The weapons seemed to be of great quality. If only they weren't made to kill the innocent, then they'd be even better. Remus and Clayton also thanked Parla. With that, we were all dismissed to go gather our forces.

CHAPTER 52

We trained vigorously over the next few weeks, becoming accustomed to our new weapons. By now, Izac was able to shoot with decent accuracy, albeit not stellar, and Dame could attack without throwing Izac out of the basket. There was once a near accident with Dame's hefty swords, giving Izac a close haircut. Now that Izac was finally back in action, his mood had lifted once more. Clayton and Remus sparred regularly, teaching eachother everything they knew. While Clayton was wise and had a fortune in combat knowledge, Remus was faster and had better control of his weapons. This made for a good educational dynamic for both of them.

While they trained with their practical weapons, I practiced controlling my skills in different environments. Priests would throw moldy fruits and hunks of dirt at me while I swatted them away. Once I was comfortable doing this, I would attack a sparring dummy while defending myself from projectiles. This eventually evolved into fighting three soldiers at once, with rocks being tossed at me from multiple angles. From time-to-time, Parla would come and watch, which subconsciously made me push harder. I know I could never beat him, let alone kill him, but sometimes I'd imagine what it'd be like to swipe that ignorant bastard off of his feet.

We had amassed a rather large army, but it was full of virgin warriors. Young men treated this as a form of glory, joining the army. They were eager to become war heros, all thinking they'd make it back safely. Given their lack of training, nonexistent combat experience, and arrogant cluelessness, I doubted many of them would make it back. These men didn't even come close to comparing to the force we invaded the City of Scaf with, but they would have to do.

    Knowing Parla was willingly sending so many of these borderline children to their deaths pissed me off, but there was nothing to be done. I had given up on arguing with him.

    Starfli and I were kneeling at the foot of Parla's throne. Parla informed, "Four days until we launch our attack. I've sent scouts out, who should be returning tomorrow morning, which is when you'll leave. They'll chart a path for you to take up until the jungle. Traversing this with an army is going to be hard, which is why I'd advise bringing extra equipment to set up camps along the way. Four days should be plenty of time to reach the jungle. Don't underestimate the Talithians. They know their home like the backs of their hands, and have taken care in domesticating multiple dangerous animals. I'm entrusting the rest to the two of you. Understood?"

    Starfli and I both stood up, nodding in agreement. I wasn't sure how we were supposed to cover that much land with any army in such little time, let alone this one. I had a feeling we'd either arrive late, or arrive with some fatigued soldiers. Even a single day extension would help, but Parla waived that idea.

* * *

I laid in my bed, staring at the ceiling. Tomorrow we marched, most to our doom. I had heard tales of the Talithians and their hospitality. They were always made out to be a very passive, kind race. I still didn't understand why we needed to kill them, other than to satisfy Parla's bloodlust. He was the God of Wrath, after all.

CHAPTER 53

Starfli and I stood on a podium in front of our men. Standing just below us were the polemarches, which were made from Starfli and I's closely trusted warriors. I hadn't met any of her polemarches, but they were veteran fighters that I had to respect. Some of them had even fought in the Old God Wars, like Clayton.

I looked out at roughly 85,000 infantry units and 5,000 cavalry, along with squadrons lugging cargo wagons behind them. Due to less restrictions and involuntary service, nearly every boy and man in Parlania was here.

The scouts had apparently found us a path that the wagons could get through, which was hard to believe. Starfli nodded over at me, her blonde hair shifting slightly in the wind. I hated her morals, but I couldn't help but find her attractive. Before I could study for too long, General Starfli gave the mark to start marching. I mounted my horse, who I had learned to half-ass ride in under a day, and led Parla's army to war.

* * *

Less than three hours in we already had a problem. Some of the recruits couldn't keep up, causing them to fall out of their ranks and mix with others. We had about an hour to go before we would even be able to see the more intense grasslands, meaning this would be a much bigger problem over time. The exhausted rode with the cavalry, which slowed them down a little, but there was nothing else to be done.

Starfli and I rode side-by-side at a slow speed, not talking until now. She spoke up out of nowhere, "Who do you think we'll go after next?" I wasn't sure what she was asking at first, so I sat silent.

She continued, "Listen, I don't like it any more than you do. But what can we do? You know, maybe Parla is right, maybe we need to kill these other Gods, that way they pose no threat to us. I'd rather attack randomly than wake up with smoke in my lungs and battle in my ears." Realizing what she was asking, I answered, "My money is on Helena. She had almost all of Parla's foot army killed all at once. Even if she doesn't attack us again for killing another one of her children, I'm sure he'll use it as an excuse to attack them next. Although, I'm not sure just how he plans to do that, given we have no way to get up there."

Starfli seemed surprised, "Oh, so you don't know then? I figured he would've told you, of all people." I shot a silent glance over at her, waiting for her to explain. My fellow general continued, "The Talithians, they have access to the clouds. The Hub Tree, have you heard of that at least?" I shook my head, having not heard of this.

"The Hub Tree is supposedly where all life began. Its roots reach to the deepest depths, and its branches to the clouds. When the Sun God Armen and the Moon God Arlen found Lewot, they first landed atop The Hub Tree. As they did, they brought the day and night cycle to Lewot. This confused the other two Goddesses inhabiting Lewot, being the Goddess of Life, Zinc, and the Goddess of Death, Ziatha. Zinc and Ziatha unearthed themselves from the roots as Armen and Arlen made their way down the branches. They met on the ground, becoming close friends." I cut Starfli off, "How in the hell do you know this? The Gods have scrubbed history clean, killing anyone found with any knowledge."

Starfli warned, "Which is why you'll tell no one of this. That's a story for another day. Anywho, as I was saying, the Gods met each other. These four were known as the Primal Gods, and they quickly became friends. They swapped tales from their homelands, talking of the cosmos and Lewot. It didn't take long for love to set in, and for children to be born. From Armen and Zinc were born three gods, all with their own powers. Arlen and Ziatha did the same, birthing two. These children spread out across Lewot. The Primal God Zinc gifted all of these children with humans, as toys to play with and watch. While some Gods treated their toys well, offering them blessings and fortune, others gave them plagues and predators. For years they lived in peace, that was, until the Gods decided they wanted to play a game. They pit their humans against each other, gambling their Godhood on victory. Alliances were made, along with other baby Gods for failsafes, who were also gifted humans and hidden away. As time went on, these second generation Gods fought and fought, refusing to lose their Godhood. The cycle started when one of the second generation Gods refused to give up their power after losing. In a fit of rage, he was killed, his power being stolen. Realizing this was no longer a game, the Primal Gods interfered, trying to stop their children from killing each other. In return, the Primal Gods were overwhelmed and killed. Their souls were imbued with The Hub Tree, as all of the God's souls do when they die. This made it so that Lewot didn't lose anything when a God died, other than the God itself. While Armen and Arlen died, the sun and moon persisted. Even though Zinc and Ziatha were slaughtered, humans and Gods alike still were birthed and died. This cycle continued: Gods fought, had kids, their kids fought, and humans were viewed as toys to kill with. Hundreds of Gods have been born and died since then, all being trapped in The Hub Tree."

    Thinking I had caught on, I piped up, "So Parla wants to take The Hub Tree to obtain all of their powers?" Starfli corrected me, "No, if that was possible, The Talithians already would have. Souls imbued with The Hub Tree can't be excavated or used. However, Scaf showed us that souls can still be manipulated, but now that he's dead, we won't ever learn how that can happen. Parla wants to capture The Hub Tree to gain access to his parents, who he also plans on killing. Parla wants to be the only God left alive, mimicking those who came before him."

My heart sank. I was a God, what did this mean for me? Starfli mentioned, "Don't worry, there's nothing you can do about it. If I were you, I'd play the part, and die when Parla has no use for you. It'll keep you alive for some time, and let you explore Lewot more than most will ever be able to. Enjoy your Godhood while it lasts."

By now we had reached the grasslands, meaning it was time for a short break. Platoons stamped down patches of grass and started small fires, cooking food from the cargo wagons. Starfli bid me well, leaving to meet with her own polemarches, telling me I should do the same.

Chapter 54

I sat with my men around a fire just big enough to cook our vegetables. They fashioned new armor, which was very intricately designed, resembling their high status. Dame and Izac offered to go hunting to get us meat, which they defined as "real food", but Clayton informed us that any animals were long gone due to our thunderous marching. Everyone, me included, was bummed that all we had to eat was bread and hot veggies.

We ate from wooden bowls instead of our armor this time, watching the new recruits struggling to find surfaces to eat on. Those with spears made simple kebabs, while the others just ate their veggies raw in their hand. Those who were smart cooked them and then used their chest plates as a plate. I'm glad we had this luxury now, as needlessly dirty armor would make us look unprofessional. I ate my hot, mushy carrots and stale bread quietly, listening to my men talk about how they thought the raid would go, looking out at the grasslands.

The tall grass spanned as far as the eye could see, rippling in the light wind. It was an hour or so past noon, meaning the angled sun bounced off of the rare trees and rocks, leaving sparse shadows. We had been here before, but I still enjoyed the view. My only wish is that it wasn't under such a morbid circumstance.

Once we were finished eating and poking fun at the new soldiers for their goofy antics, we met with Starfli and her group. We mounted our steeds, and Starfli blew into her horn, signaling it was time to gather our things and continue on. After waiting a couple of minutes, we set off. I looked back, noticing a few soldiers struggling to hurry and fall back into ranks. I wasn't sure how we could ever invade the Talithians with this group, losing more and more faith as the hours went on.

It didn't feel like long before night beset us. We couldn't travel the grasslands at night, as torches risked wildfire. We could get away with campfires after stomping and pulling the surrounding grass, but even then, the radius had to be big. Stray embers could be devastating, hindering our army by days. Instead, we set up our tents and settled down for the night.

Chapter 55

I woke up in my own tent, which was an odd feeling. Remus and Clayton stood outside, guarding me as I slept. I must have woken up before the march, otherwise that familiar, annoying bell would have shaken my cot until it broke, forcing me awake. This gave me ample time to eat and change my clothes.

I sat alone around a sputtering, dying bonfire, lightly heating some corn over it for breakfast. Once I was done with that, I returned to my tent, nodding to my guards, then entering. I swapped my toga for under armor, then put my full set of armor on. The second I placed my helmet on my head, the bell rang, signaling it was actually time to get ready.

*   *   *

Starfli and I rode in front of our army once more, for what felt like about an hour now. Feeling well rested and much more talkative than yesterday, I started today's conversation. "What do you know about Modus? I hear a little about a few Gods here and there, but nobody seems to care about Him."

Starfli thought for a moment, not sure how to word what she was about to say. Once she found her words,

Starfli explained, "Modus is an interesting character. He's the father of this generation of Gods, as I'm sure you already know. What isn't talked about is exactly why He's the God of Nothing. I can't say I know much either, other than He was once a very powerful king. He ruled over a large mining operation, supplying the world with ores and valuable gemstones. He was a pacifist, which led to His downfall."

I asked, "Which was?" Starfli, still unsure exactly what to say, answered, "You remember how the Gods were supposed to give up their powers when they lost? There's a chance they don't need to lose to give them up. My dad speculated maybe He gave his powers up to protect His people, but I'm ultimately not sure." I concluded, "Ah, so that's why He's called the God of Nothing, He has no really Godly powers? I thought it was just slander, or perhaps He was just strong and didn't have anything else to Him." Starfli added, "I wouldn't say He isn't strong. We don't want to underestimate Him when He ends up on Parla's chopping block." "If He doesn't have any Godly powers, why kill Him?", I wondered out loud. Starfli answered with something that made me think. "Because He's still a God, and that scares Parla." I inquired "What do you mean He's scared?"

Starfli concluded, "That's enough for now, speaking ill of Parla sounds like a terrible idea." I agreed, continuing, "So, how do you know all of this?" Starfli seriously shot back, "I don't know anything. This conversation doesn't leave your mouth." I made eye contact, nodding, showing I understood.

* * *

We finally reached the woodline. We had to stop twice, once for a large group of pitiful soldiers demanding rest like children, again for a wagon full of food breaking an axle. These accounted for nearly an hour of wasted time, which greatly annoyed us high ranking fighters. We had two days to get to where we needed to be, and the hardest part of the journey hadn't even started yet. I dreaded dealing with these whiny kids once we reached the jungles, even more so in jungle combat. I also had heard complaints about ration sizes, which I brushed off. Once half of our army was dead, there would be plenty of food to go around.

CHAPTER 56

Another day had passed by, which proved to be much less successful than the last. We were now deep in the woods, following the path that Parla's scouts had laid out for us. The army had made about half of the progress they should have today, which had us generals and the polemarches in a horrible mood. It'd undoubtedly annoy Parla that the invasion was going to start late, but ultimately, there was nothing we could do.

These woods were an unfamiliar beast, full of new noises, smells, and sights. Deciduous trees surrounded us, the sun filtering through the high leaves and long branches. Birds chirped and called far ahead, being scared off by the massive army. Starfli or I would occasionally see a deer or small game for but a second before it ran off into the safety of the woods. The ground was covered in stray leaves, multiple kinds of ankle-high grass, and ferns. There apparently were also thorn bushes here and there, as a polemarch would sometimes ride up and inform us of a soldier refusing to continue through this "hard terrain".

The sun finally started to set on the day, casting shadows on the forest floor. The further in we went, the denser the flora. It got so humid that I had to slow my breathing down to stop from sweating. Once we could no longer see, Starfli blew the horn to signal it was time to set up camp. As she did, flocks of hidden birds from all around us scattered in every direction. That is, all but one.

I kept my horse still, looking deep into a crow's eye. Its head was turned sideways, allowing us to focus on each other's pupils. It wasn't a staring contest, but a warning. Starfli rode up beside me, asking, "That's weird that one didn't fly away. Maybe the crows don't mind the noise?" I continued to stare at the dark bird, waiting for any movement. There was something I was missing. I wasn't sure what, nor why I felt this way, but there was more to this crow than it was letting on. Starfli pulled me out of my trance, "Hey, are you still there?" I brushed the feeling off, nodding.

* * *

Once camp was set up, I joined the polemarches and Starfli for a combined effort dinner. We ate less than last night, trying to preserve food for the journey back. That was, if we made it back. I still felt unfond of the men that followed me that I didn't already know.

After a light serving of stale bread and ale, we all turned in for the night. My men were so annoyed and done with the newbies that they didn't even have a burping competition, and just wanted to get some sleep, which I didn't blame them for. After they solidified who was in charge of the night watch and when, everyone turned in for the night. We had a long ride ahead if we were to make it into position by tomorrow evening.

* * *

    The day had begun like every other since we had set out from Parlania. We were extremely deep into the woods, so much so that it turned into a jungle. New kinds of trees and plants surrounded us, their rare, unique colors contrasting the otherwise solid green. The humidity made the air taste like it was sweating, which was an unfamiliar experience that I'd rather never have had. The bugs were terrible, flying through the eye slits in my helmet. I'd have to quickly take my helmet off, pick the bastard off of my face, or worse yet, out of my eye, but this was often hindered by bugs biting at my face and neck. Without a full suit of armor, this would've been even worse.
    We marched slower than ever, as soldiers had to ride out ahead and clear the brush for the masses to get through. If there was ever a reasonable time to complain, it was now.
    We were about 15 miles away from our target location when the sun set. It got darker on the jungle floor than it did in our native land. Since the trees already blocked so much sunlight, now that there was hardly any, it was basically night. Just as I had predicted, we weren't going to make it in time.
    Suddenly, Starfli held up her hand, signaling for us to stop. Something was wrong. I didn't realize how loud

our marching was until we had stopped moving. The only thing to hear now was our breath and the horses' micromovements in the tall grass. Torches lit up the jungle, although we still couldn't see too far in.

    I asked, "What?" Starfli pointed ahead of us. The cleared foliage had suddenly stopped. A helmet lay at the end of the trail, which marked the beginning of another smaller clearing, like someone had been dragged through the grass. She looked over at me worriedly. I yelled back to the polemarches, who would send out informants to the rest of the army, "We've been had! Tell everyone to keep their heads on a swivel!" I couldn't see their expressions through their helmets, but I could sense their concern. Listening, they rode out in different directions.

    Starfli took her sword out, looking every which way, swinging her torch around to force the night back. Being as quiet as possible, I scratched at my wrist to draw blood, making it so there was no delay in the event I'd need my own weapons.

    Suddenly, the leaves shook. Not from plants on the ground, but above us, in the treetops. I looked up, Starfli helping me see by hoisting her torch to the sky.

    That same crow from earlier sat above our heads. It watched me, almost like it was studying my soul. I couldn't break eye contact with it, there was just something off about it. Starfli muttered, "What in the fuck…", casting her torch straight ahead, the shrubs moving slightly.

Striking swifter than lightning, a massive jaguar jumped out, tackling me off of my horse and onto the ground.

CHAPTER 57

Before I could act, the jaguar tore through my shoulder plate and into my arm, rendering it useless. I wasn't the only one ambushed, hearing battle happening behind me as well. I felt the cat's serrated teeth carve into my shoulder blade like it was a juicy roast. Yelling, pinned to the wet jungle floor, I was in too much shock to react. The jaguar began to wrestle with my arm, effortlessly tearing it out of its socket and casting it aside.

It reared up to pounce on my chest, which would surely kill me. I intercepted the attack, shoving my hand forward, forming a sword in its neck. A guttural growl escaped the beast's mouth, along with its last breath.

I shoved my entire body against the dead animal, forcing it off of me so that way I could get up. I looked over at my mangled arm, then my disheveled stump. It wasn't just my arm that was missing, it had torn out most of my left side collarbone and shoulder blade. All I could do was scream in agony, trying to stay on my feet. I was dizzy, losing blood at an incredible rate.

I had to calm down, or I'd die. I tried to slow my breathing down to slow my blood flow, but that was hard when undergoing such trauma.

I called upon a tentacle to bind my lacking limb, since I wasn't going to stop my bleeding on my own. I looked back at my army, seeing their dropped torches starting brush fires. More massive cats, along with muscular apes and predatory birds tore men in half, making quick meals of them. All I could do was watch; I wouldn't be of any actual help in this fight with only one arm. I couldn't continue deeper into Talithia, that'd be a death sentence. Before I could plan my next move, something wet and scaly swiftly knocked me off of my feet.

    I grunted as I hit the floor, but wasn't able to regather myself before a snake wrapped around me. It was an enormous boa constrictor. The weight of a thousand bricks crushed me, stealing my breath. I tried to use my tentacles to tear it off of me, even apart, but it just wouldn't work. I had spent so much energy trying to live through the pain of a grisly amputation, there wasn't any strength left for me to fight back. The thudding steps of a bulky, silver ape neared. Defenseless, it kicked me in the head.

    Black.

Chapter 58

Through blurriness I could see multiple entities standing around me. While humanoid, they weren't really humans. Dazing in and out of consciousness, sweltering pain engulfed my body. What was happening to me? Where was I?

Once I finally awoke, I was in an foreign place. The room was only lit by the sun shining through a hole in the wall made to look like a window. Everything around me was made from wood, only not crafted. It seemed as though somebody had carved this room out of a tree, which was rather impressive. My missing arm felt heavy, which was odd, considering it was no longer attached to me. I pushed through the burning headache I had to look over at my arm, only to see it had been replaced by some sort of contraption.

Before I could really study it, a fair looking Elf waltzed through the door, moving gracefully towards me. I knew Her face, I just couldn't pin a name to Her in my mental fog.

Sitting on the edge of the bed, She said in a light, elegant voice, "I really didn't think the animals would have captured you. While they haven't ever disobeyed us, we figured that they might kill you just out of spite. I'm glad to see that they didn't"

I studied the Girl. She was young, slim, and fair looking. Long, white hair rolled off of Her shoulders, and

Her bright green eyes scanned over me. Her voice had a sort of warmth to it, an innocence.

I asked, "So why didn't You just kill us then?" She giggled, stating, "Oh, we killed as many of you as we could. You were coming for our heads, after all. Unfortunately, a few of you got away, the forest fire set up a boundary. You were the only one I wanted alive." It clicked in my head. "So that makes You Seebes?", I asked, already knowing the answer. Seebes looked surprised, questioning, "Parla really tells His people of the other Gods? I really didn't think that'd happen, given His love for censorship and smear campaigns." I nodded slowly

"Well, let's cut to the chase", Seebes said, "You've been kidnapped, clearly. Believe it or not, this isn't out of malice. I had heard tales of the young God of Blood and his prowess on the battlefield, and wasn't looking to pull any punches. If we had only taken you, the invasion would've continued anyways. The reason we took you was to open your eyes to Parla's evil, and hopefully help My Mother and end His massacre. However, that can wait until you get better. Rest, gather your strength, and when that's done, I'll tell you the truth."

With no other option, I nodded once more, signaling that I understood. As Seebes left the room, I fixed my gaze back to the ceiling.

I really didn't understand what this false arm would be good for. Surely it couldn't replace my real one? Maybe it's some sort of custom the elves had? I couldn't be sure until later.

What about Parla? I knew He wouldn't just let me be taken as a prisoner of war. But, after the Talithian's display of battlefield advantage, what could He do? Most importantly, what about me? What was Seebes going to show me? When She was done with me, would She kill me? There were hundreds of questions flowing through my mind, keeping me awake for longer than I would've liked.

    I knew that the first step in getting back to Parlania was to pull myself back together, which meant resting up for the journey back home. I touched my forehead, feeling the wrapped wound from getting punted. Blood coated my fingers, giving me a realization. Before I could even finish the thought, He pulled me into his weird alternate plane of existence.

    I looked across the shallow sea of blood, staring at Parla. He marched towards me, grabbing me by the throat. I didn't even feel like fighting back. Parla hoisted me into the air, screaming, "You idiot! This is quite literally the worst possible outcome! How the hell do you plan on getting back to Me? What good is My warhorse when it resides in another stable?" I couldn't interject, as I didn't know the answers. He dropped me, kicking my chest.

    "Almost a third of the men I sent with you died, and it's all because of you! One of my best generals, along with thousands of veteran and new soldiers alike, gone! Why don't I just kill you now?"

    I made a weak attempt to stand, coming up with a lie on the spot, "Because I'm inside now. I don't need anybody else to make this work. Hell, I just spoke with Seebes a mere minute before You pulled me here. She's going to take me somewhere to tell me what She says is the truth about You." Parla lost some of his heat, but the fires of rage were still burning inside of him.

"I would have much rather you led my forces against the woodland creatures, then continued your invasion. It would've kept My army looking much healthier, and Starfli alive. While a costly plan, I know you'll make it work. If you don't, I'll just have to stop your heart. I want you to meet with Me regularly, so that I know you aren't lying to Me. Understood?" I concluded, "Yes, I understand."

As the final words escaped my mouth, I was put back into the bed. I couldn't just kill Seebes. I had to learn more about Talithia to plan a successful escape, on top of needing to hear this "truth" She had to offer. However, I couldn't take too long, or Parla would flip his killswitch on me. Whilst plotting, I slipped into slumber.

CHAPTER 59

A few lethargic days passed by before Seebes had decided I was ready to get up. I had spoken to Parla the night before, telling Him I planned to kill Seebes within the next three days.

Two armed Elves put me in shackles while Seebes told me, "Just because I want to befriend you, it doesn't mean that I trust you. I'm sure you understand" I stood up, following Her out of the room. I was led down a set of stairs, then outside.

This section of the jungle was much more lavish than the part I had been in. It seemed to be separated into three major parts: The jungle floor, the branches, and the treetops. On the floor, it was pretty dark. Shadows were casted by the massive tree limbs overhead, but that didn't stop the Elfs from their busy days. Beasts of all kinds hauled big carts of food and resources around, some even flying above me, delivering products. It was similar to Parlania, but had something unique. Everyone here seemed happy, enlightened even. It wasn't just a few stray smiles here and there. People excitedly conversed, talking about any and everything. Children ran around, playing with their large pets and any flora they could get their hands on. This must be what happened when you ruled without vitalizing fear.

I wasn't even looked at by anyone. I'm sure they knew who I was, they just didn't care. They knew they were safe, and this life that they had was going to last. I couldn't imagine that peace of mind, living fearlessly and in harmony with one another. I envied it.

I must have been right earlier about the trees being hollowed into buildings, seeing as how people walked in and out of them. Shops, housing, restaurants, everything seemed to be inside of one of the massive jungle trees. The architecture was admirable, massive swirling patterns engraved in the outside of the trees, then painted over with the brightest color palette one could imagine.

Seebes called my attention, "Hey, have you figured that arm out yet? It saved your life, you know." I said, "No, I guess I haven't messed around with it." Seebes explained, "Well, it's quite easy. We have some tubes running from that arm's fingertips straight to your heart. I don't know exactly how your Godly powers work, but I figured maybe it could work. I know it isn't the same as a real one, but maybe it could be made native to you."

Surely enough, with the right blood manipulation, the arm went up. It was pretty heavy, as it seemed to be forged from solid steel. I flexed the elbow, but didn't have too much freedom to tinker with it given my chains. While it wasn't my own arm, maybe I could make it my own.

I followed Seebes and Her guards all the way to the base of a tree that was somehow bigger than the others surrounding it. Seebes stopped, looking back, "I know you know what The Hub Tree is, as I heard that Starfli girl tell you about it through My crow." Well, at least that bird was finally explained. Seebes continued, "I'm not sure how she knew all of that, seeing as how she came from one of the most censoring Gods to ever walk Lewot. Anywho, everything she said was true. However, she failed to give you some of the more recent stories."

      Seebes continued into the bottom of The Hub Tree. Unlike the others, this one wasn't marked with designs or paint. I assumed this was due to it being sacred. Roots wove beneath my sandals, making a sort of bumpy flooring on its exterior. Its lowest branches scraped the underside of the treetops. It had to have been over 3500 feet tall. As we entered, I noticed there wasn't anybody else inside. Glowing bugs the size of my hand lit the room up, showing the only thing on the walls were empty canvases. As we made it to the back of the room, I noticed a single portrait. It was of Scaf.

      Seebes explained, "See, The Hub Tree never used to be this big. It actually used to be hardly top 100 feet. However, with every death, it needed to paint another picture of the fallen to hold their power. With every new generation, a new floor was added, meaning that it had to grow. Now that hundreds of generations have passed, it extends so far up that you can almost see everything Lewot has to offer. However, I don't need to take you up that far."

      We went up a flight of stairs, seeing more portraits of fallen gods. Two of the fifty-ish canvases here were empty. I assumed these were for Modus and Helena. Seebes continued, "Now, as you may have noticed, there are a lot more portraits here than the floor below. The truth is that Parla killed every single one of these Gods here. They were his Uncles, Cousins, and other Family, as you know. Scaf was the 56th God He culled. Now, that is no small feat, I'm sure you know that."

I nodded, baffled that Parla had so many heads strung to His belt. It explained the "Wrath" portion of The God of Blood and Wrath. Seebes turned and stared into my eyes, "Now I want you to imagine what He could do with the power of The Hub Tree. This power, in reality, isn't untappable, it isn't as though He couldn't steal it. The only reason those that came before Us haven't is due to the understanding that it's sacred, and The Hub Tree would surely fight back against such an action. Parla doesn't care about this. He wants to steal every single power He possibly can from here, which is why He's so eager to kill His kin. You know, Scaf didn't attack Parlania first. Parla sent a party to poke at their borders, throw threats out, and they were killed. Parla then called that an invasion, declaring war on The House of Scaf. He didn't even need to do that with Talithia, He simply ordered an attack. He wants to take The Hub Tree, and use that to combat Modus and Helena, since he knows he can't fight them without it. He doesn't have the power to walk the clouds, nor to even try to kill Modus."

I asked, "Then how did I walk on the clouds when Helena captured me?" Seebes answered, "Well, My Mother can control the cloud's density, even to weaponize them. I'm sure She probably just hardened the clouds under your feet at the time, as She wanted you to be there." Next, I asked what has been burning away in my mind for quite some time now, "What is so special about Modus?"

Seebes answered my question with another, "Would a God give their power away willingly if they knew their warlord Son was coming to kill Him?" "Well, no." I replied. Seebes explained, "Well, that would be the case, unless He knew He didn't need it to destroy anyone who stood in His path. That empty portrait over there might not have any picture since He isn't dead, but it still holds His power. While My Father might not have any Godly powers, He doesn't need any to burn this world. Just because He could, it doesn't mean that He wants to. To prevent this possibility of massacre, He took His few people into a ravine to live a hermit's life."

Everything had made a little more sense with this new knowledge. I had always known Parla was evil, but I didn't recognize this was His plan. If I helped Him, it would be the end of Lewot, but if I didn't help Him, I couldn't try to stop Him later. I couldn't do this on-the-fly act anymore. I needed to plan meticulously, or the world could end with me.

Chapter 60

I was led back to my room, being told I'd be released the next morning. If I was to act, it would have to be tonight. I couldn't just wander around Talithia, I'd surely have eyes on me at all times. If I waited for night to come, I could perhaps find Seebes and kill Her. She had given me the information I needed, and served no purpose to me. I had to kill Her to please Parla, or He'd be suspicious of me.

Two meals were delivered to my room before dusk, which both consisted of grand salads and grains, but no meat. I supposed they wouldn't eat meat, given they coexist with these animals. This explained why the Elves around seemed so small; they ate like cows, grazing on their fancy grass.

I spent my time relaying the story I had pieced together thus far, really taking in how horrible of a tale it was. Peaceful Gods met each other, and grew to harbor a very real love for one another. They had families, and created what was a beautiful world, at the time. Inventions and competitions were made to entertain the Gods, to keep their lives feeling fresh. This devolved into murder and power-vacuums, leaving death and devastation behind for no real reason other than boredom. This continued for generations, down until my own.

The reality of the situation was that not every God had even wanted this, and even actively took measures to avoid it. Modus, for example, giving His power back to The Hub Tree, or Seebes, Who wants to help me prevent this cycle from continuing. On the other hand, others, like Parla, fed the fire. It was Gods like Him that made the Others act out of fear, creating more chaos and tragedy. He had to be stopped.

CHAPTER 61

Once the cover of darkness had fallen under the treetops, I got up from the bed and tried the door handle. To no surprise, it was locked. I then looked out of the window, seeing I had a substantial fall below me. I had to find a way down that wouldn't give me away.

I looked around the room to see what materials I had. The vases were stuck to the table, as everything was carved from the tree. I knew the shrubbery in the vases and pots around the room wouldn't do me any good. I couldn't use the blankets as ropes to lower myself, as people would surely see the white silk draping out. Other than that, I didn't have anything at my disposal. I scratched my head with my metal arm, getting used to using it. With this action came my escape plan.

I called upon my sword, running it against my steel fingertips. They took some time to sharpen into claws, but it ultimately worked. Putting my sword away, I pricked my finger with each claw, making sure it was pointed enough to gouge into tree bark.

Hoisting myself up into the windowsill, I stabbed my fingertips into the wood. Surely enough, it stuck tightly into the tree. I looked down, noticing that the ground suddenly seemed much farther away than before. I did my best to dig my feet into the wood, just for some extra support. My normal hand hung me from the window, moving the new one as low as I could, jabbing my fingers into the wood again. I let go of the window, plummeting down. My arm held true, leaving me dangling from the side of the building. Now that the light from the window wasn't on me, I could take my time descending.

I grabbed onto an artistic carving in the side of the tree, pulling my metal attachment out. I fell lower, just above another window. Letting go, I grabbed onto the windowsill. To make sure that no one in the room had seen me, I pulled myself up enough to peak inside. It was luckily empty.

Taking a deep breath, beads of sweat rolled down my face. I was almost to a point in which I could drop down. After repeating the process of sticking my claws into the wall and lowering to a windowsill or carving, I dropped down about 8 feet from the ground, having some shock sent through my legs, falling over. I stayed laying down in the dark, looking for elves in a prone position.

Massive bugs flew around rather slowly, their abdomens lighting up and illuminating the empty streets. The shift in social activity from day to night was impressive, given I couldn't spot a single elf.

Moving slowly, I carefully avoided making any noise. I wasn't even entirely sure where I was going, all I knew was that this had to be done tonight. I steered clear of roads, sticking tight to buildings.

I followed the height of the trees, figuring it'd make sense for Seebes to reside in the tallest, excluding The Hub Tree. As the treetops grew higher into the sky, I started to get complacent. I'd kick a rock, stand a little taller, or even move faster. Before long, I simply walked, only being cautious of the bug's light. The city was, oddly, completely dead.

					*			*			*

I knew it was where I needed to be the second I had laid eyes on it. Within eyeshot of The Hub Tree, another grandiose tree stood tall, branches sprawling out in every direction, connecting itself with countless other wooded towers. At the center of these branch bridges was undoubtedly Seebes's residence. Rather than being painted with bright and iridescent colors, solid gold coated each crevice in the bark, solidifying that it was an important point of interest in Talithia.

I stood around 150 feet away, crouched and hiding behind a small well, presumably used to water the horses in the nearby stable building. The same bugs flew on multiple levels, now on leads being held by guarding Elves. Their light gleaned off of the silver Elven armor, making them seem as elegant as ever. There were about 50 guards, but that was only what I could see from the exterior.

With no obvious way in, I had to scope out the area. The only ways to get in without being seen would be a window. However, guards standing at every corner made it seemingly impossible to get there. Perhaps I could make a distraction big enough to pull just enough of the guards away to get in?

    Glancing over at the stables, I took notice of a few elegant steeds. Each of them were pure white, and built like a lumberjack. While they were standing, they were still, signifying they were at rest. The stables were about 15 feet to the left of me, and the road was around 5 feet to the right. Ahead of me were the interwoven trees, and behind me the empty town. A fence would offer me minimal protection if I was to make my way to the stables. Seeing no other option, I got down into my belly and crawled as slowly as possible, moving only inches at a time.

    Grass that had grown up around the base of the fence was my only cover. If I had moved too fast, or a guard came around, I'd surely be spotted. I stopped crawling to occasionally check my surroundings, making sure that nobody was looking near me. Just as I was less than an arm's length away from the stables, a light began to grow up my side.

CHAPTER 62

I couldn't look behind me to see what was happening, but I had known there was a light bug illuminating my feet. The clinking of armor chain links slightly broke the night silence, warning me that I was about to be caught. I sped up my pace minimally, careful to not make any noise. I could touch the stable wall now, pulling myself forward, careful to not disturb the grass. The light came closer and closer, with the footsteps close behind. Just as I rounded the corner to be out of sight, I heard the footsteps halt.

There was a clattering of armor, then a small hiss of falling liquid. The guard had only come over here to relieve themselves, and I had almost been caught because of it. Not risking them taking the corner and finding me, I turned another corner, still moving slowly, and entered the stables. Crouched down, I rested my back against the wooden wall, letting out a very quiet, but deep sigh. Had I been caught, I likely would have been killed.

Once I heard the guard put their suit back together and walk away, I looked around for any new angles on the situation. Six snoozing horses stood in separate stalls, all with hay and water. I took notice of the leads, rotating my mental gears. I very cautiously undid the ends of the ropes attached to the stables, being as careful as I could to not wake them. Littering hay around the stables, I left myself a walking path to avoid any noise.

Nabbing a horseshoe, a flint knife from the tool bench that was used when changing horseshoes, and another handful of hay, I made a small trail around the back of the stables, then out to the taller grass that guarded me by the fence. This grass was rather dry, perfect for burning.

Scattering little bits of hay here and there, I made it back to the well. I glanced around, making sure no one would be close enough to hear the first few strikes of my homemade flint and steel. I held the blade at an angle, pushing it away from me off of the horseshoe. The first few strikes gave me sparks, but not enough to start the grass on fire. With no success, I took a short break to check my surroundings once more.

There was a light breeze now, which made goosebumps rise up my arm. It felt as though they raised up my replacement arm too, but I knew that wasn't possible. Phantom pain was something that was going to take a bit of getting used to.

With my first returning strike of the flint, enough heat was made to start the grass on fire. I lightly blew air into it, the gentle breeze aiding me. Once the embers were big enough, I looked around, saw no one was looking my way, and ran to hide behind a small vendor booth.

The booth was made from the same wood as everything else. I had assumed it was a produce station, as the bins were empty but smelled of sweet fruits. Laying down, I watched my flames spread from a distance. It took a while for anyone to notice. As the orange speckles crawled down the fence line, they suddenly stopped. Rubbing my forehead, I came to a terrible realization.

The fire stopped spreading right where the guard had urinated. The wet grass was stopping the spread, causing the small flames to die down. Rubbing my forehead, I figured my plan had failed. However, in a fortunate turn of luck, just as the fire had almost disappeared, the light wind carried over some embers and ashes to the next patch of dry grass, lighting that on fire.

Warmth flooded over me, followed by relief. Once the fire wrapped around the back, all of the dry hay went up in a matter of seconds. Before I knew it, the horses whinnied and dashed in every direction, jumping the fences and scattering every which way. A few guards yelled out, exclaiming that there was a fire. Leaving their bugs behind, soldiers dipped their silver helmets into the well, tossing water on the swiftly growing fire.

I saw my chance. The front door opened, and out came around 20 Elves. Wide open for my sneaky entry, I stealthily crouched, yet ran, over to the heavy door. The second I stopped inside, I was bewildered.

It was gorgeous.

Chapter 63

  Golden etches made extravagant spirals and swoops around paintings of nature's beauty, slightly glowing, helping the lanterns brighten the massive rooms made from light colored wood. Furniture was carved out from the tree, rendering it immovable. However, I wouldn't change a thing about the interior. A grand spiral staircase wrapped around the outside of the room, leading up to other thick branches that made for what I assumed were quarters and studies. There was a reception desk on this floor, but there was no attendant.

  My sandals clacked on the polished floor. Looking down, there were too many rings to count; I couldn't begin to imagine how old this tree was. Entranced to waltz behind the front desk, I couldn't help but allow the artwork to mystify me. I froze when a voice echoed, calling down to me.

  "I knew you were coming, but the fire was bold, cunning even. You should know you can't go back once you do this.", Seebes's soft, green eyes made contact with mine as She descended the stairs, Her gleaming hair dragging behind Her. My heart jumped into my throat, not allowing me to respond. Seebes stood a few steps above me, Her hand gently resting on a guardrail, continuing, "You confirmed My suspicion, you can talk with Him at will. Interesting trick. So, you're here to kill Me, but I just can't figure out why…", She trailed off into thought.

I answered with uncertainty, "I'm here to put an end to all of this. If I need to cut a finger off to save the hand, so be it." Looking up at me again, Seebes stepped towards me slowly, "You don't know where you stand either, do you? You've come all this way, and you still can't decide what you want?" A level of hostility and disappointment set in as She dug deeper, "You've seen more than any other mortal has, and even most Gods at this point. You know what's happening, and you still aren't sure what decision to make?" I interjected, "I know what I'm doing!" Brushing me off with laughter, Seebes continued, losing Her aggressive tone, "You're a boy, I should've expected as much. It's unfair, the fate of this many left up to you. I take pity on you, Dylan."

Taken back a bit, I asked, "How do You know any of this for sure?" A smirk was given to me instead of an answer. Seebes concluded, "Go ahead, whatever reason you're doing it for, this ends with My death. I can only hope you walk the correct path from here."

My mind muddled, an answer sunk into my head. Parla, no, the God's madness had gone on too long. If I wasn't to do something, who would? As if She knew what I was thinking, Seebes nodded her head, "A worthy sacrifice I'll make, I feel. You know how to do it, just don't make too much of a mess. I don't want My people to see me in too bad of condition, please."

It made no sense, not why, but how She could offer Her life so easily. She knew it was for the right reason, but to do it so carelessly? I reached out, grabbing Seebes's forearm, making a prick in Her wrist. Before I could do the job, She spoke Her final words, "Dylan. I believe in you."

CHAPTER 64

Those words struck a chord in my heart that I wasn't aware existed. Never, not in my entire life had I heard something like that. Seebes soft eyes slowly lost their soul as I siphoned Her blood into my arteries. Setting Her down carefully on the staircase, I owed Her the kindness of a comfortable resting place until She was moved to Her permanent grave. A single tear rolled down my face. Why did this life feel so different to take?

Knowing that it wouldn't take the guards forever to return, my feet guided me out of the tree, then the village. While my initial approach was stealth, running was the only thing that interested me now. That single tear teased out its family, making my vision full of hazy colors. I hadn't cried since leaving home, if I could even call it that. Traveling on pure autopilot, millions of thoughts all rushed in at once.

Why me? Out of anyone, why couldn't my parents have loved me, both the fake ones and Parla? How could someone be so evil as to breed and beat another, their own son even, into being a personal war harbinger? Why did I have to be entrusted with a few soldier's lives, let alone everyone that lives now and after me? None of this was fair.

Once there wasn't any light left to go off of, I slid and sat, resting my back on a soft, rotted log. The greenery made for a pleasant cushion. Wet moss dampened my back as I sank into it. Curling up into a ball, I couldn't take it anymore. I had to cry quietly, or they might end up hearing me, which would mean all of my progress would've been in vain. My lungs hurt, heaving out heavy sobs into my crossed arms.

All of my thoughts formed into one singular one, being a morbid truth. I wanted to die. Sitting here, I wanted it to be my final place. Muttering through broken cries, I whispered, just to hear myself say it, "I want to kill myself. I can't take this anymore, it's too much." I repeated this for what felt like hours, my eyes swelling from crying so hard. Occasionally wiping my faucet of a nose off on a stray leaf, I couldn't calm down.

The muscles in my stomach cramped up from the soul-crushing exertion. Still in a ball, I laid down on the moist forest floor. Without knowing it, I dozed off into a somber, yet well needed, sleep.

CHAPTER 65

Warmth crawled up and over me, slowly waking me up. I lay in the damp moss, which in turn made my clothing slightly cold and caused it to stick to my skin. Swelling and irritation made my raw eyes hurt whenever blinking, meaning I had remained crying in my sleep. I hadn't remembered laying down in the moss, only sitting up, but it wasn't unlike me to roll either.

The moss had proven to be a comfortable bed. Standing up, I didn't feel even slightly sore. My only complaint was that the jungle was incredibly muggy, making me put in an effort to breathe. Shade was cast over me and nearly the entirety of the ground, smaller animals skittering around in the shroud.

Knocking the only thing on my agenda off, I looked around for something I could use to make myself bleed enough to speak with Parla. I started by digging a small hole in the muddy soil, then filled it with saturated bark to make an earthen bowl. I then cut into my wrist.

It hurt terribly, but I just couldn't bring myself to stop. Focusing on the self-inflicted pain, my mind was cleared of any issues. I kept scraping away at my forearm, tearing apart my muscles and tendons. Blood first dribbled, but gradually started to overflow my homemade container. I could stop and speak to Parla now, but I didn't want to. From my palm to my elbow, I sliced my skin to ribbons. Suddenly, the first words in a few minutes seeped into my mind.

"Dylan, I believe in you." That was my sobering thought. I stopped, shaking my mental numbness, looking at what I was doing to myself. I had one good arm, and I decided to carve it up? What an idiot I was. My hand was almost entirely limp, the pain of minced flesh starting to aerate, helping Seebes' words. I dunked my head into the pool of dirty blood, closing my eyes and waiting.

In an instant, I was transported to the endless blood ocean of Parla's. He stood still, looking at me and my mangled arm. In a calm, yet impatient voice, "Well?" I answered, "I did it to mys-" Cutting me off, Parla stated, "I don't care that you hurt yourself. What I care about is your progress. Is She dead?"

My heart sank. He couldn't find room in His shriveled heart to care that His own son, albeit distant and a simple plaything, had hated his existence so much that he'd tear his arm apart the way a shark would its prey? Anger and misery flooded my mind once again. Loved by nobody, my only reason to live was to save those that didn't even care to take a second from their day to wave at me, let alone give a damn about me. Maybe they weren't worth it, maybe I should let them all die and free myself from this hell.

Parla snapped His fingers a few times, "Hello? Still there? Did you kill the Cretin, or no?" I nodded my head, a tear rolling down my cheek. Parla looked at me confused, cocking his head and squinting in borderline disapproval as he marched towards me.

"Excuse Me, am I missing something? Are you here to snivel to Me like a useless puppy, or lead My armies? What are you going to do, cry? This isn't who you were raised to be, you know better than that, boy!" I muttered, clenching my fists as I looked down, "What do You know about raising me?"

Parla stopped, an amused look resting on His smug face. "What was that?" Looking up, I let it loose, "I said, what in the fuck do You know about raising me?", A grin grew across Parla's face as I continued, "You're no father of mine, nor are You the great leader You think You are. You hide behind hostages and lies! You aren't anything more tha-" Parla yelled at me, "Watch what leaves your mouth next, boy!"

Taking no heed to his word, I finished my statement, "Parla, You're nothing but a Coward."

Chapter 66

As the last word escaped my lips, a wake of blood rippled around Parla's pounding feet. He attempted to grab my throat to ridicule me, but I grabbed His outreaching hand with my fake arm instead, using myself as a fulcrum to swing Him over my head. A splash of crimson rose as the God fell, streaking across my clothes.

I knew He would give me no time to recover, so neither did I. I called upon my tentacles to grab His arms and legs, but they were grabbed and countered by tentacles of His own. "Insolent fool! Insulting and then attacking Me! I'll kill you, boy!"

Using His blood tentacles to throw me by mine, I tried to stop my fall with my human arm. However, it instead sank down into the blood, which had never happened before. As I pulled it back up to reveal it as completely healed, Parla said, "Cowards take unfair fights. I'm not a coward." I retorted, "Cowards lie to Their sons and use them for Their own twisted biddings!"

With my arm okay again, I called upon my familiar sword, taking a battle stance. As our tentacles grabbed, slapped, and tore at each other, us Gods ran to the other. Rage overcame me and powered my first strike. My sword swung diagonally, attempting to break through His collarbone. A tentacle took the blow for Parla, intercepting my sword and then disappearing into the Owner's back.

Parla followed this by extending His arm straight out, a spear forming to jab into my abdomen.

With a near escape I was able to jump atop the weapon. In an instant, Parla called His weapon back, His tentacle grabbing my ankles before I could fall, hanging me upside down.

Pissed, Parla presumed, "So, you've decided that since you aren't on top of the world, you get to be an emotional brat?" That wasn't my reason at all, but I didn't have time to worry about that. All of my tentacles were pinned by His, stopping them from retracting or aiding me.

"Keep in mind you're a slave to Me, boy, nothing more than a tool for My wars. Killing you here and now would be a loss to My campaign, but if it needs to happen, I'll do it. Tell me, will you submit?", Parla berated. Instead of answering, I called upon my blade by my achilles tendon, cutting through one of the tentacles holding me. In a swift movement, I caught the falling blade and hurled it towards my Opposition's face.

This break in concentration caused Parla to drop me headfirst into the shallow blood below me. While He tilted His head to the side to avoid death, the sword still made a deep gash into His left cheek. Blood dribbled down at first, but soon sucked back into His face, followed by His tentacles. I stood up, ready to fight again.

Parla faced me with anger in His eyes, equal only to mine. I insulted once more, "For the God of Wrath, You sure seem to be a pushover. Here I was thinking You were some skilled Fight-" Cut off once more, Parla shot a sharp, red projectile out of the palm of His hand and at my face. I ducked, hearing it wizz overhead. I had never thought about trying to conjure other weapons, perhaps this was the time?

Thinking about what I should try, a single tentacle of mine split my back open again, offering a glaive. I had never used one in combat before, making this a worse idea than it initially had seemed. Parla cared not for this, calling all of His blood conjurations back to Him.

Offering a final olive branch, Parla said in an oddly calm and welcoming tone, "You really don't want to walk this road. Without Me, where would you turn? What do you have without Me?" Thinking rationally, without Parla I had nothing. However, I had nothing I wanted and everything I hated due to Him. I answered honestly, "You know, I'd have nothing. I'd lead the normal life of a peasant, working until I eventually dropped dead from some sickness or died in war. But, You know what? I'd rather that than being some, what did You call me, a horse on Your chessboard? I don't want to be anyone's piece to use. I want to control myself. If patricide towards Someone Who was never a Father to me anyways is how I take my control back, so be it."

Parla smiled, "Alright, at least you know what you want. I'll give you this boy, you're smart, and a force to be reckoned with. Any other would've given into being My little horse on the board, or they would've died already, but not you. You have grit, and certainly aren't weak. But, you forget something." I raised my eyebrows to acknowledge that I'm listening.

Suddenly, my feet sunk into the blood below, trapping me. Walking towards me, Parla continued, "You forget that you don't have the choice. While you're a natural born killer at heart, you'll never come close to reaching My level. I mean, could you even comprehend how I pull this off?", gesturing to the shallow ocean of blood around Him. The blood stuck to my ankles like quicksand, refusing to let me go as Parla walked towards me, continuing, "You have incredible power, but you haven't had the time and experience that I do to develop and master it. You've only recently learned how to control it, but Me? I was born in this blood, molded by it, but you wouldn't know what that's like."

Chapter 67

"I mean it, I was torn from My mother's stomach during wartime. She had been beheaded during an invasion by My Uncle. My Father, Modus, used His bare hands to rip her open, dug through her guts, and grabbed Me. They thought I had drowned in her blood, but my Father carried me off regardless.

It was a shame, really. My Father had apparently quite the establishment. Millions of men, women, and children willingly bowed to Him. While He had the capacity to wage immense and terrifying wars, He often conserved Himself. That was what had led to His downfall; Others conspired behind His back, knowing that He'd seek out peace. Once a treaty was signed, His guard was down. Then, before anyone knew it, Modus' kingdom was in flames. The fact of the matter was that His Siblings wanted His power, and that's why He gave it up in the end.

Anyhow, He managed to escape with Me in tow. We slept in a cave for a prolonged period of time, living off of any animals He and His remaining personal guard could get their hands on. The cave slowly turned into a home for Us. We mined and mined for precious metals to try and evolve once more. Life slowly began to get easier, and I grew into my Godhood. Before I knew it, I could manipulate the blood of the game we killed to strengthen Myself.

By this point, the metals and gemstones He had mined grew into and under His skin and that of those around him, turning them into beastly abominations of ore. Becoming masters of tool smithing and monstrously strong, they had nearly resembled Gods themselves. However, Father was always weary of My power, advising Me to get rid of it. I knew why, as His powers cost His then-wife and kingdom. But, I knew that unlike Him, I had the stone heart and iron fist to wield it like a Ruler. I refused to give up my Godhood the way He did, and that was met with an ultimatum. Give My Godliness up, or leave.

So, I left. I mystified smaller tribes with my power, recruiting those that feared Me, and making examples of those that didn't. I had taken My knowledge of minerals and mining from the caves and applied it to the nomadic tribes ability to hunt, along with the more stationary tribes farming techniques. Passing skill sets around, we had the ability to create what started as a small village, which grew into Parlania. As time and generations passed us by, Parlania grew into what you know it to be now.

In the meantime, Modus grew His mining economy and married once more, to Helena, having My sniveling Siblings. As a sign of respect, My Father gifted Helena an offshoot of the cave. There, they found a precious mineral that changed colors with the time of day that was so buoyant it could float even in the air. Like Modus, Her and Her people slowly became covered with this rock, gaining buoyancy themselves, and even carved themselves to look like dragons and other aviary beasts. Those flying serpents you see? Those are humans that carved the stones stuck to them and took years of practice to control the ability to fly. Helena hardly has any real Godly power, but is recognized as One due to pure luck.

So, remind Me as to what your qualifications are to take My place?"

Chapter 68

New information about the Gods had always shaken me a bit due to the atrocities involved, but nothing quite like that. I realized how Parla grew to be the God of Blood and Wrath. "You know, sure, You had some tough shit go on. But how can You let that define Who You are? You're doing the exact thing now that created all of Your problems to other people.", I reasoned. Parla responded, "No, I'm killing any God other than Myself to break the cycle. Once there is only One, it can never happen again. I won't let you get in the way of that."

The blood that held me still let go, allowing me to step back up to the surface. The glaive sucked back into me as my heart rate slowed and body temperature leveled out. Taking another attempt at reason, I informed, "You know, it seems as though You're the only One out for blood right now. Scaf never attacked first, and Seebes had intentions of making peace, even up to the point that I killed Her. Modus hasn't emerged in decades, and Helena only came down to try and stop You from needless killing. You really have no reason to kill Anyone anymore." "That's what They told My Father. Anyways, sob story aside, you're to find your way back to Parlania. I'll have troops marching outside of the woodline to bring you home, but it's up to you to get back to them.", Parla said before dismissing me.

Gasping in the disgustingly thick air, a bug shot down my throat. After coughing and hacking like a chainsmoker, I checked my arm to see it had healed, just like in the vision. Was it even a vision, I wondered? He was right, I really had no idea how that worked.

I knew there was no way to reason with Parla, but I had dug deeper than anyone had before into His head. Maybe, just maybe, I could find a way to get the remaining Gods to gain His trust and end these wars? That'd require a hell of a lot of work, but if it could stop any future bloodshed, it was worth a shot.

Looking up, I could hear, but not see, the rain. It took some time before the water filtered its way through the treetops, streaming off of foliage everywhere. The forest floor quickly turned from squishy moss and soft dirt into mud splotches and puddles, making walking rather annoying.

I couldn't retrace my steps from yesterday due to the precipitation, but I could go off of my memory. Given that I ran here before, walking back in less than savory conditions was going to take some time. When close enough, I could circle around and hopefully find some indicators of where the woods were, and from there I could look for smoke and burned trees, which would lead me back to Parla's scouts.

* * *

As I trudged back, my clothes got heavy. I ended up taking my sandals off and carrying them, as the wide bottoms proved to be more of a hindrance than anything when picking my feet up from the mud. Animals holed up in trees, avoiding the elements and looking down at me. I had to be careful for any sort of predator or bird, as they could be scouting for my presence. The mud caked all over helped conceal me, but you never know.

Storms persisted for hours, showing no sign of letting up. I couldn't see the sun through the thick treetops, so it was hard to tell the time of day. Noon would make sense, but completely relying on intuition wasn't the best idea.

I stopped for a moment to rest, thinking about climbing up the first branch of a tree so that I didn't sink in the mud due to stagnancy. I jumped, slamming and using my claw arm to dig deeply into the trunk. Using my other arm, I grabbed up further, as the lowest branch was at least double my stature. Hardly able to grip the limb, I took a deep breath and held on tightly. Doing a one-armed pull-up, I swung atop the branch and took a few deep breaths. Animals scurried away from the noise I had made, meaning they luckily weren't watching out for the Talithians.

Once I had regained my stamina, I mindlessly continued upwards, repeating the process that I did to get here in the first place. As I got closer to the top, everything beneath me lost its detail. The wet bark would occasionally make me lose my grip, giving me a few close calls. The trunk got thinner with the air, my heart rate slowing to match the lack of oxygen. I had been climbing for minutes that had felt like days now, the jungle floor below me almost invisible due to foliage. Wiping the rain from my face, I looked around to see if there was any sight of the sky. Instead, I was met with a sudden movement.

    Tracing the movement and minor sound with my eyes, I couldn't find the source. Staying still, I scanned the area. From the corner of my eye, a large, black splotch jumped from tree to tree. I was being stalked.

CHAPTER 69

I stood on a thicker branch, about as wide as my feet. Since I was higher up, limbs had gotten thinner and more abundant. Not wanting to be caught off-guard, I called upon a second set of claws, that way I could grab onto the tree or attack any opposition. I figured it'd be much like hand-to-hand combat, so surely they wouldn't take much practice to viably use.

Continuing to look around, I heard a couple of shakes in the leaves and thuds. I was being circled, stalked. Yelling out, I taunted, "Alright, c'mon you bastard!", to no avail. Standing still for a few minutes, I eventually let my guard down. Maybe it was just a few birds trying to sneak away from me. I kept going up, pushing past any muscle fatigue in my upper body.

The thought had nearly slipped my mind until I saw another sudden movement. The branches were hardly big enough to stand on, and certainly were too small to be comfortable on. I'd have to revert to only hanging and climbing pretty soon. Taking a moment, I waited for another movement. Below me this time, I saw what looked like a tail for a split second.

I knew that I was being followed for certain now, refusing to move on until whatever was near came out. Looking around, I couldn't see the jungle floor whatsoever, but a few rays of sunlight came through, acting as a natural spotlight on the green leaves.

What they failed to cast light on was a gigantic black cat that jumped at my feet, yowling. I was just fast enough to escape the grab, but its sharp and lengthy claws still grazed my leg, shallowly cutting it open. I pulled myself over the branch, wrapping myself around it. The cat landed on the thicker branch that shook viciously with its weight.

A few drops of blood dribbled down on the jungle cat's head before I reminded myself to slow the blood flow near that area. It looked up at me, hissing and growling. I had been made, as this was in close resemblance to the Talithian cat I fought earlier. Not wasting time, I made myself a crimson pike and swiftly jabbed downwards into the stalker's face, hearing a slight yelp and the crashing of breaking branches as it fell out of sight, ragdolling across limbs. The sounds became more faint. I continued up. I was now on a time crunch, and a deadly one.

It took me only a few more minutes of climbing to reach the top, the sun starting to set now. I stood up, a foot on two separate branches a little lower down, holding tightly to the top of the tree trunk. I looked out at what seemed endless.

Ahead of me were taller trees that were likely Talithia, glowing against the coming darkness. The sun falling behind Talithia, casting pinks and oranges that climbed overtop of each other, staining into the clouds and remaining sky. The rain was gone, a calm and chilly breeze the only notable weather oddity. I could see my breath here, showcasing my altitude. To my left and right were endless trees, showing how sparse these woods really were. However, to the back left of me, there were pillars of smoke that billowed up, along with a blackened area of dead trees. I could hardly see it, but I knew there was a fire there that must've been reduced to embers.

    I took one last deep breath before making my descent, a new target in sight. Trekking Eastward, I had around a day's walk ahead of me, maybe two. I couldn't stop for too long, as the Talithians would mob me if they caught up.

Chapter 70

Getting down from the jungle giant took about half of the time that climbing up did. All I really had to do was stick my claw into the trunk and slide down a few branches at a time, rather than the seemingly endless amounts of pull ups I did earlier. Once I was at the bottom, cold mud climbed up to my ankles, entrenching my feet. Slopping and sloshing noises accompanied by bird calls followed me as I walked Eastward.

*   *   *

Moving around in the complete darkness, I took it slow. I didn't want to fall down any slopes or run into any sort of predatory animal. With uncertainty in my steps, all I could really do was go in what I thought was the correct direction, using the occasional dimly-lit firefly as my only guidance.

After what felt like an hour of walking, I threw the towel in. The ground hadn't lost any of its saturation and I was extremely fatigued, mentally and physically. Feeling for any sort of tree, I eventually found one that I could get up and into.

With some trial and error, I managed to scale to the first branch, which was luckily thick enough for me to sit on. I propped myself up against the tree trunk. Using my tentacles to wrap myself tightly to the tree, I shouldn't fall out.

There wasn't a difference between opening and closing my eyes with how dark it was. Not a single thin ray of moonlight could shine down at the ground, or even illuminate the leaves well above me to give them a glow. The only thing to hear was my breath, the ribbiting of frogs, and the rare happenstance of a bird fluttering their wings to change tree limbs. It was eerie here, yet peaceful.

Given I had stopped now, it would make sense that I'd be back to the burnt woods late tomorrow night. Once the sky was open, so long as it wasn't cloudy, I could get to Parla's scouts. Before more passage of time, I was out like a blown candle.

Chapter 71

Cold rain poured down onto my head from a leaf above me, startling me awake. The sudden panic made me lose my balance, falling over the edge onto my stomach. With the air shoved from my lungs, I gasped, soaking and covered in mud. Standing up, I muttered, "Goddamn son of a bitch...", wiping my mouth and eyes while I cussed at the circumstance. With an aggravated sigh, I continued forward. I'd occasionally stop under running streams of water made by large leaves overhead to clean the mud off of me and get a quick drink.

With a ruined mood and a wonderful start to the day, the only thing that pushed me at this point was spite and pure ambition, emboldened by annoyance and rage.

* * *

The crow was following me again, despite keeping a rather swift pace through the rough conditions. I had tried to throw balls of mud to hit it a few times, but that was foolish and had no payoff.

The shrubs and trees were starting to get shorter, but the storms persisted. At times clouds would peek through the leaves, showing my progress. Even the mud pits started to get shallow. The sun was seemingly going to set soon, as it was slowly getting darker and darker, meaning I had to be getting close to where the fire was.

Hearing a crunch behind me, I stopped abruptly. The midnight black crow followed suit, its gaze stuck on me like glue. Turning around, I saw nothing unordinary. But, I was smarter than this. Shaking up the formula, I turned the ends of my hands into crescent-shaped ax heads. If there was any more stalling on my end, I'd end up caught. Bolting away from the thick jungle, I realized my sandals must've gotten lost in the mud after I fell from the tree, which was fine by me.

Controlling my breaths, I kept my heart at a steady pace to keep myself from swift exhaustion. While I couldn't hear any pursuers, I wasn't about to stop and listen. The rain died down to a light sprinkle, and I came out to a sudden clearing.

Ashes mixed with precipitation on the ground, making a gray soup. Trees were without any leaves, and any foliage was now a crumpled black husk of its former beauty. Embers rarely sparked, popping. However, the rain had killed most of them. The sky was as clear as it could be, a few thin gray clouds passing by. Stars shone above, accompanied by a full blood moon that lit the dead woods up just enough for me to see where I was going.

I stopped for only a moment to take in the sight, but couldn't for long. Picking my pace back up, the wet ashes felt gross on my bare feet. Still ever so slightly warm, soot stuck to everything it touched on me, still toasty, but not enough to burn me. If not for the rainy weather, Talithia likely would've had a massive problem on their hands. Well, other than a dead Queen.

A branch hidden by a puddle turned into a mush under my pounding steps, still hot enough to make me yelp. Halting to frantically swish my foot around in the puddle to get it off of the soles of my feet, I heard a plethora of wings flapping and footsteps beating on the ground, possibly paws too.

With no time to waste, I sprinted again. Yelling out for help as loud as I could, I prayed Parla's scouts could hear me. After wiping the rain from my face a few times, I gave up on calling for help. The sounds got louder and louder, the forces behind hunting me like a dog. I had a sudden thankfulness for the slow newcomer soldiers, as that meant I wouldn't have to cover as much distance due to them not making it too deep.

With the animals right on my heels, I took a quick glance backwards. Wolves, bears, cats the size of wagons, hawks, there wasn't a single animal behind me that didn't want my flavor. When not paying attention to what was ahead of me, my shin connected with a fallen, burnt out log, tripping me. I landed on my stomach, stumbling to get up and run again, but the hawks dived on me first.

Ripping chunks of flesh from my body, the attack sent shockwaves of pain through my body as the birds cut into me with their beaks and talons, making it impossible to get up. I swatted up in the air, running an ax blade right through a hawk's neck. I couldn't get up.

Rolled over onto my back, animals would soon overcome me. I screamed in fear and agony, the biggest of the hunting party nearing. So close to my goal, maybe another fifteen minutes of running and I would've made it out. I lashed out whenever I could, slicing and even killing a few, cries of pain matching mine.

I heard the heavy paws approaching, the other assailants clearing out. A bear the size of a house approached me, its paws bigger than the average shield. The blood red moon made it cast a shadow over me, emphasizing the monster's size. The bear reared up on two legs, getting ready to slam down on me. Doing the only thing I could at this point, I readied two wall shields to try and survive the attack.

Not watching, a thwack, followed by deep growl came from the bear's direction. Peaking out, the bear had reared back, an arrow lodged into its side.

Confused, all I could do was crawl backwards, disgusting water slopping into my wounds. Whatever loosened the arrow had to have been behind me, as I couldn't see anything from where I was. Then another came, striking a hawk from the sky. Running footsteps splashed in puddles, clinking armor nearing me with grunts of effort. I feebly stood up, looking all around me to see my cries for help weren't for nought. A force of around twenty men threw themselves at the fauna ferociously, cutting them down with minimal opposition. A few archers sat back, picking off their numbers.

However, the bear had a mission. Rushing me, I stuck a shield up, using my other arm to brace against the blow. Once contact was made, I was thrown well backwards, landing on my back again. Another arrow sunk into the bear's flesh, this one into its left paw. With no time to waste, I got up again, even if weakly.

The bear swiped at me, but I used a tentacle to grab the oncoming paw, stopping it. Using my own claw, I swiped across the bear's face, ripping the right side of its head open. With a loud groan, it backed down, another arrow striking from above and landing in its back.

With a bellow loud enough to break glass, the bear turned tail and ran, followed by the few remaining predators. I fell down again; not even the animal blood I absorbed enough to keep me up. Passing out, my job here was done.

Chapter 72

For a while, although I'm not sure how long, I bobbed in and out of a dizzy haze. With aches and pains everywhere, every bump and jolt hurt. Why I was being moved around, I wasn't able to figure out. There wasn't much thinking capacity left in me, only a need for rest. Snippets of conversations could be caught around me, unintelligible, seeming to take place far away.

The intervals of consciousness started to become more frequent, words starting to make more sense. With this, I also felt my fatigue and damages more clearly. Every chunk of flesh torn out of me had a burning sensation, likely due to an infection of sorts. Rough stitches held the bigger wounds closed, clearly done by a non-professional. I hurt all over.

In a moment of lucidity I heard a familiar voice. For some reason I associated it with crying, or grief, even though there was a relieved tone to the young male vocals. I took note of my surroundings, although the light had burned my eyes. Through a squint I could see that I was in a Parlanian tent, which offered incredible comfort. The tent flaps parted, and a familiar face approached.

"I'll bet you've got one hell of a story to tell, don't you?", Remus said in a comforting voice, "We were starting to wonder if you made it. Well, I suppose that you almost didn't. By the time we even got you into the cart your heart rate was near non-existent. I was the one that ended up patching you up, which I'll apologize ahead of time for. I've only ever seen it done, never taught how it's done, y'know?"

I appreciated Remus' care, he needn't apologize to me. Who knows, maybe his makeshift first aid care is what put me over the living side of the fence. I wanted to thank Remus, but I didn't really have the strength.

Continuing to talk my ear off, Remus explained, "Those birds did a surprising number on you. It was similar to uh, what do you call it? Death by a thousand paper cuts? That sounds right to me, anywho, they pulled off so much of your skin and little chunks of you that you actually came close to bleeding out. Wouldn't that be a way to go? The God of Blood, well, kinda, dying to blood loss? You know-", Remus was cut off by the next person entering the tent, which was Clayton, "Well I'll be damned, he's up! You were really starting to scare us there, son."

All I could really do was listen as they talked, as I didn't want to tilt my head to look at them. Instead, I did my best to simply move my eyes to them. I was tired. While I was grateful for the care I was given, rest was desperately needed.

Remus and Clayton blabbered on, and I tuned them out. Slowly but surely, my eyelids blanketed my eyes, putting me back to sleep.

CHAPTER 73

As the next few days passed by, a group of around fifty men hauled what was left of me back to Parlania. Without an arm, a few pounds of skin and flesh, and a rather immense amount of blood, I was certainly not in the best condition. Remus was right; I'm going to have one hell of a story to tell once I'm back.

Nights and days all felt the same while I came in and out of sleep. I had no idea how many days it had been, nor how long ago I was saved. My only focus was rest and healing. Bread and water were rationed to me, even though I didn't feel hungry or thirsty. Guards convinced me that I needed to eat, and I didn't have it in me to argue.

Soon I had heard a mixture of cheers, gasps, and concern from people surrounding me. I could hear festivities of sorts, meaning I was likely back in Parlania. Still laying dormant in the cart, I didn't want to open my eyes to look at what was surrounding me. However, when the cart stopped and someone picked me up, I had to.

Dame scooped me up in his arms and took me up the palace steps, looking down worriedly at me. Hearing Parla's voice, He said, "Well, the kid made it back. An impressive soldier, that one. Take him to his room, I'll send My servants to care for him." Dame responded, "Yes, my Lord, of course."

Closing my eyes again, I felt as I sunk into the soft silk sheets and comfortable mattress. This was significantly more comfortable than that musty cart. For a few days priests and priestesses came in and slit their wrists open over me, allowing me to take their blood in for my strength. This remedy helped bring me back to a more permanent state of lucidity.

The sun shone into my room, sounds of average commerce taking place outside. A priestess knocked on my door and came in. "

Sir Dylan?" she said, "I'm going to need to take those stitches out now. You've fought off most of the infection, and your wounds are starting to heal over. We figured we'd better leave your new, erm, accessory, on and let you decide if you'd rather your arm to regrow, or that."

I slowly peeled my blankets back. "Yes, I think I'd like to keep this trinket arm. It shows my conquest of Talithia.", I told the priestess. While that wasn't completely true, it's what I would tell people in order to keep Seebes' gift. I could still hold my blood weapons in it if need be, and it could function as a claw on its own, why not keep it anyways? The priestess complied as she walked to my bedside, "Of course, Sir Dylan." She had a small knife in her hand, ready to cut the stitches. I shied away a little, given anytime any sort of blade was near me it was to hurt me.

Taking note of this, the priestess reassured, "I'm only here to help Dylan, I promise. Now, please stay still for me so I don't accidentally cut you." I studied the priestess as she pulled my stitches out. She had dirty blonde hair, and wasn't much older than me. With deep green eyes she reminded me of something, but I couldn't quite put my finger on it, given I still had a slight fogginess to my mind.

Pulling a string out of my arm, it stung a little. The priestess made small talk, "So, how'd you do it? Kill Seebes, that is." I lazily replied, "With civility, if I'm being honest. She knew She couldn't fight me, so I took it easy on Her. However, I'm not sure that's the story the public will hear, so that stays between the both of us." The priestess nodded, cutting the next stitch on my upper chest and pulling it out and continuing, "Of course, Dylan. I have to ask, what was She like? I've heard a range of stories making Her out to be some Swamp Hag, all the way up to the most Beautiful Thing in the forest." Again, with maybe too much honesty, I answered, "She was a rather fair Maiden. I'd certainly say She leaned more towards the Beautiful side than the Swamp Hag. She seemed pleasant, as a Ruler and a Person."

Taking a stitch out of my cheek, the priestess replied in a mildly heated tone, "If She seemed so pure and special, why kill Her?" Sensing a sudden hostility, I warned, "Hey, do you have an issue or something? Watch how you talk to me." In the blink of an eye, the priestess' blade was on my throat. She whispered, "Make a noise and I'll gut you like a pig and leave you on this shithouse's steps."

CHAPTER 74

Connecting the dots, I realized that this must've been a Talithian. The assassin continued, whispering, "That's right, you've been had. I followed you barbarians back to this disgusting place just to kill you for my Queen. But first, I want answers." I could feel her seething between every word, a very real pain in her voice, "What makes this place worth serving? I mean, look around you for once. The poor are forced to join the army, otherwise they are publicly shamed. Alcoholism and blatant tyranny. Parla cares not for any of you. Hell, they cut themselves open just for his pleasure just outside. There isn't a single redeeming quality about this trash heap, so why? What do you see here that I don't?"

The attempt was valid, but the assailant must've not taken into consideration that I could control my own blood, and that slitting my throat would do them no good. However, I humored them, "You know, you're right. I can't argue anything that just came out of your mou-" Being cut off, the Talithian raised their voice to a normal tone, "Then why did you do it? Why did you kill Her?"

Complying once more, I answered, "Because I don't have the option. Either follow orders, or Parla kills those close to me. I'll give you the honest truth, seeing as there's no chance you make it back home alive. Parla took who I thought was my family hostage, killed them, then used that as an excuse to conscript me. I'm His son, and

I've inherited His powers to some extent. I killed Scaf the same way, only because if I didn't the few people that I cared about would've been shamed and executed in front of crowds of peasants. I'm trying to make a difference here, but to do so, I need to play into His hand a little."

The tiny knife pushed harder onto my throat, "So you're a coward then? Killing because you're scared of what'll happen?" I answered plainly, "What decides if I was a coward or if I was a hero will be the outcome of my life. What I think matters not, only those that come after me." The Talithian waited for my explanation.

"I know it might not seem like it, but I'm trying to uproot and usurp Parla. I've learned that He is the only one in this generation with a need for war, and it's only because He's scared. He wants to be the only God left, meaning it'll be me on the chopping block once I'm done doing His dirty work. I'm trying my best, but I'm just as scared as He is. The amount of lives that rest in my hands is terrifying, and I don't know what to do. I'm sorry for your Queen, I really am. I'm sorry for any of those animals we killed, and I'm sorry for the power vacuum that I likely left behind. It was my only option."

In a moment of thought, I could tell my assassin-to-be was off their guard. Wasting no time, I punched through their chest with my claw hand, feeling their sternum and ribs shatter around my arm. The knife was dropped and landed on my chest. Not instantly killed, the imposter slumped on my arm, choking on their blood, which entered through my own wounds.

I assured, "I'm sorry for this too, but die knowing that your Queen will be avenged, even if it's the last thing I do."

Chapter 75

Yelling out for help, guards and priests alike stormed into my room within seconds. A spear flew through the Talithian's throat, spraying blood all over me, finishing the valiant woman off. I had a respect for her, coming all this way for answers and vengeance. It further showed how important Seebes was to her people. Making sure I was okay, a familiar priest asked, "Sir Dylan! Are you okay? Have you been hurt?" I shook my head no and ordered, "Check the grounds for a dead priestess. She had to have gotten these from somewhere."

A few guards listened and ran out to search. Peeling the woman off of me, the guard hauled her out of the room, all of the blood leaking out of her crawling up my bed and to me. I stood up, a few entrails and bone fragments in my hand, along with on my bed. I set them down, ordering the priest, "I think it goes without saying that I could use some new clothes and sheets." With only a mild muscle fatigue now, I walked out and down to the baths.

I sat down, enjoying the steamy environment and hot water. It felt good on my achy body. Contemplating everything, I thought, *"I really hurt a lot of people in killing Seebes. When this is all over, I need to make sure that the Talithians are cared for. If I ever rule, I should take notes from them. I need to kill Parla before anything else happens to any innocents."* I closed my eyes, running soap across my chest.

"Maybe something could be learned from that assassin. Who ever said that I had to fight Parla? I can't kill him in a fair fight, so why give Him one? Maybe I could slip into His room at night and cut His head clean off. No chance for regeneration or a mistake, just a decapitation. Would it really make me a coward if I was doing it for the good of everyone? I really don't think so", I pondered while washing my hair in the soapy water.

Getting out of the toasty water, I nabbed a towel and dried myself off. I realized that I somehow wasn't even sure where Parla slept. However, that couldn't be too hard to figure out. That's what I will do tonight. I'll take today to regroup with my friends and figure out where the Bastard sleeps, then, under the night's cover, I'll kill Him where He sleeps.

After getting dried and dressed in a new toga, I returned to my room to see that it had already been tidied up. A nice platter of cheese and crackers had been made, which I snacked on. Looking out of the window, I could see that it was midday. It was busy outside, people shopping and conversing.

Once I was done eating, I walked out to the throne room to see Parla in His usual place. Coming out of a slump to sit forward, His fingers weaved and elbows sat on His knees. Parla eagerly asked, "Well, how'd it go? I see you're healed, even despite an assassination attempt.

Even I haven't undergone one of those; you must've really mangled my Bitch Sister!"

Disgusted with Parla's excitement, I told Him, "I did what you told me to do. That's what matters." Leaning back, bored with my answer, Parla teased, "You really need to work on your storytelling skills. Enjoy life as a God, live a little. The people here love you, they think you've saved their harvest from the evil Seebes' oncoming famine magic. Of course, that's a lie kept between us." "Sure.", I replied, walking out.

Walking out I thought, *"Don't worry Parla, you'll have your assassination attempt."*

Chapter 76

Making my way through crowds of pedestrians that congratulated and thanked me for what I had done, I found myself at the Red Inn again. The same small bartender from before came out. She nodded at me, "Sir Dylan. Coming in to escape the masses?" "That, and to find my men. Same room as last time?", I responded. Nodding, I could tell she had dealt with semblances of war heros before. I appreciated her not bombarding me with adornment that I ultimately didn't deserve.

Trotting up the stairs and down the hall, the Red Inn seemed rather quiet today. I noticed it had always been pretty tame, especially for housing soldiers. It was pleasant. I knocked on the door to the room, to which Dame opened. Excitedly, he welcomed, "Guys, it's Dylan! He's alright!" Dame opened the door wide, ushering me inside.

Everyone wore a happy expression. Izac was laying down on the bed throwing a ball up in the air and catching it, Remus was sharpening his sword, and Clayton was writing something down in a notepad with his quill and ink. All of their attention turned to me, seeming to be happy that I was alright.

Remus and Clayton stood up, coming over to me, "Well, let's hear that story then!", Remus eagerly demanded. I sat down at their table. Dame picked Izac up and set him in his own chair, then found his own, along with the other two.

    I had to lie to them, as no one could know of Parla's deception or it'd end up with them in trouble. Telling only partial truths, I explained, "Well, the Talithians kidnapped me. They offered me hospitality in hopes that I'd change sides. I played along for a while and healed up, Which is how I got this.", saying as I moved my arm to show what I was talking about. I continued, "Then, I snuck out, went to the second biggest tree, then started a fire. This pulled all of the guards out. Then I snuck in and killed Seebes. After that, I ran away as far as possible, making my way back to the burnt woods. But, as you know, their animals found me. I only lived due to the Parlanian soldiers coming just in time, and even then, I was torn up pretty good."

    While Clayton made his way over to a cupboard, Dame asked, "Okay, but why the second biggest tree?" Before I had a change to answer, Izac piped up, "Because she wouldn't be living in The Hub Tree, you oaf. That's sacred ground, you can't live there. That, and I've heard the trunk is too thick for them to carve homes out of anyway." Dame muttered, "Your mother sure likes my thick trunk." This got a little giggle out of everyone, except Izac, who retorted with a playful, "Oh, fuck off."

    Clayton returned with a rather thick loaf of bread, offering it to me. "Here. It isn't much, but a gift for getting us all home safe. I figured I should put some skills to use that my wife taught me, no?", Clayton explained. I took the loaf and accepted the handshake he offered after, nodding a "thank you" at him.

Figuring I'd tell them before they asked, I added, "Oh, and a Talithian snuck into my room this morning and tried to kill me. Dressed up as a priestess and came to me while I was half-awake. But, I put a hole in her chest big enough to look like she was run through by a ship's mast."

Trying to steal the joke from each other, Izac and Dame both fumbled words and yelled over the other along the lines of, "I ran your mother through with my ship mast!" They both laughed and swapped a couple baseless insults while the rest of us listened, amused.

For the rest of the night we talked about how life had been while we were apart, and what we thought was next. They all figured we'd be starting another war campaign, but unbeknownst to them, they'd be serving under someone new come morning.

CHAPTER 77

The sun was just starting to set. As I was walking up the stairs to Parla's palace, out of pure pettiness, I absorbed the blood left in bowls as offerings for Parla. He wouldn't need the strength once the sun rose anyways. At the top step, a priest was coming out to collect the offerings.

After scratching his head, he turned over to me. "Don't worry," I told him, "I've already taken care of it." The priest nodded and thanked, "Ah, I see. I appreciate your steadfastness, Sir Dylan." Just before the priest went to grab his broom and start sweeping the steps off for the night, I asked, "Oh, one more thing. I have an errand to run, but I don't know if I'll have time to talk to Parla between dropping this off and going back out. Do you know where I could find him after dusk?", motioning towards the bread Clayton baked for me as a gift.

"Well, I suppose that's knowledge that is okay for you to have. Behind His throne there is a rug with a trapdoor underneath, a rather rudimentary hidden room. Maybe don't bring up you heard it from me though, Sir?", the priest hesitantly answered. I assured, "Oh, no, I won't be doing that. Have yourself a goodnight, and thank you."

Making my way into the palace now, I saw that Parla wasn't on His throne, meaning He was likely already down in His room. Guards still stood present around the premise, offering protection to those sleeping, per usual.

Four stood in the throne room, all faces that I had seen around before. Not sure how I'd get them out, I walked back to my room. Setting the bread on my dresser, I plopped onto my bed. With around an hour to kill before complete nightfall, I made a plan.

"Once it's night, I'll be able to do something close to what I did in Talithia. I told the priest I had an errand to run tonight, which will help cover-up for the guards seeing me walk out tonight. Either that, or make me more suspicious. No, wait, that doesn't make much sense. Maybe I go out from my window instead? Then, I can find something to maybe light on fire. Yes, That'd work. Well, but what if there were people inside? What about the owners? Ah, I'll just pay them back once I'm in the position to do so. When Parla is dead and I'm sitting on the throne, I'll pay them for their losses and make a big deal about His death. That might help. I need to get in and make sure it's empty though, I don't want an innocent to die during my revenge. Once the fire has started the guards might go try and put it out. If they don't abandon their post, I suppose they might be a needed casualty, as much as I hate thinking about that. Well, I'll want my own men put into place as my personal guard anyways, so maybe that's for the best. After they're handled, I'll strike."

CHAPTER 78

Taking the last bite from the slice of gifted bread, I wondered if Clayton had even ever touched a cooking utensil before. It was tough and had odd chunks of unmixed flour in it. Hunting was his strong suit and I felt that he should probably stick to it.

The sun had completely sunk below the town, clouds blocking out most of the moonlight. The only light to go by was from lanterns and torches, which were sparse. However, at least I knew how I'd start my fire.

Slowly and carefully, I pulled the pegs that kept the window pane in the frame out. Praying that it'd fall into the palace so I could catch it, I jiggled the last peg out. With that, just my luck, the glass fell outwards. If it wasn't for the little garden bed of flowers that sat outside, it would've shattered. Looking back at the room, I took a deep breath, and hopped out of the window.

Jumping out just far enough to avoid stomping on the glass, I picked it up and put it back inside. That'd make it easier to reassemble later. Walking away from the lighting of the palace, I made sure to stay low. There weren't really any patrolling guards. That was likely due to most of the guards being at our borders, making sure there was no retaliation from Talithia.

The town square was pretty spacious, mainly for festivals and events, in the rare event we had them. Empty merchant stalls were littered on the outskirts, and behind them, novelty shops. I had never been taken here often as a child, as Mom and Dad, if I could even call them that anymore, were too busy with other things. Speaking of, I wondered how Devon was doing? I haven't had much word on him. While not my actual brother, I still cared.

I snuck across the neat stone bricks, nearing the other side. I scoped out stores, as they were the most likely to be empty. If I nabbed a torch now too much attention would be called to me. Scouting through windows, I saw a few things. Restaurants, grocery stores, woodworking shops, anything and everything. I felt bad that someone's passion and hobby was about to be destroyed, but it would hopefully be worth it.

I found my target. An old bookstore, which would surely light up easily. I felt as though this was a sin. I tried not to think about all of the history and knowledge that would be lost with this action.

I grabbed a torch and a rock. Using the rock, I prayed nobody would hear me throw it through the window. Glass loudly shattered and shot all around, giving me a hole big enough to throw my torch in. Trying to toss it back towards a bookcase for maximum likelihood of fire, it smacked the books dead on, leaving embers and tiny flames to spread across them as it fell to the floor.

Running back to my window, I swiftly crawled inside and hurried to reconstruct it. I watched outside as the flames grew, casting light out into the streets. This quickly grew into smoke billowing out of every possible hole, including the broken window. Once my window was put back together, I took a big sigh.

Focusing outside, it took a while for anyone to notice the fire. But, once one person yelled, it didn't take too much time before more joined. Two guards ran out from the palace, which would save their lives. Knowing that the time to strike was now, I walked out of my room, slowly closing the door behind me.

Chapter 79

I tiptoed down the hallway, careful not to alarm anyone. I passed by the paintings I had so long ago, stopping for a moment. I studied each of the Gods. I had seen Four of the Five now, and I could see that there were a few small discrepancies. Scaf was much bigger than portrayed here, and Seebes was a bit more angular. Helena was almost perfect, other than the shade of purple She was colored in being much too light.

Snapping out of it and getting back to business, I made it out to the throne room. To my dismay, four guards still stood here. The other two must've come from wandering hallways so that Parla could be protected. One spoke in a gruff voice, "Sir Dylan, no need to be worried. Old bookstore caught on fire. You can go back to sleep, you're in good hands."

If I told them to go help put the fires out, it'd be suspicious. Instead, I acted out of rashness. I wasn't really sure what else to do. Using my tentacles as swiftly as possible, I latched around each of their necks tightly so that they couldn't breathe. I explained in a whisper, "Your families will be well cared for, I promise. But, I can't have anyone knowing about what happened tonight. I'm sorry." I could see the panic and confusion set in their faces, along with shades of red from asphyxiation. I didn't want them to suffer without reason, so I made my tentacles push them right, then left, and then spin them in a full circle by their necks.

    I continued this until I heard all four of them snap and could see that their bodies were lifeless. I piled them up in a corner as softly as possible, feeling slightly bad for what had to happen. They hardly even got to die as men.

    Remembering what the priest had told me, I quietly walked behind Parla's throne. Sure enough, there was a red rug, and under it, a trapdoor made from a darker wood. I carefully pulled the latch up, trying to be as silent as possible. I took the metal ladder down, turning around to see a lavish room.

    Made from marble and quartz, just like everything else in the palace, gold accented each piece of furniture. There was a dresser, table, few chairs, countertop with cupboards for storage, shelves with books, and a small vanity. Most importantly, there was a large and lavish bed built into the floor. Red, silk curtains covered it, hiding who was inside. Not wasting any more time, I carefully pulled the curtains back. Just as expected, there laid Parla, asleep. I called upon my sword in one hand, then a hammer in the other.

    I needed to hurry. I approached slowly, took a deep breath, and raised my arm. *"Here we go, the end of an era"*, I thought. I dropped my sword down, cutting Parla's head clean off. A white explosion came from each end of His neck as His eyes opened, some sentience left in His last moments. Not taking any risks or asking any questions about the white blood, I used my hammer to cave Parla's skull in. At first only a small hole was made, more white blood and brain matter splattering all over the sheets. I beat into His skull, the cracking and smacking noises echoing in the underground room.

    Tears rolled down my face, knowing that my never-ending agony was over. Parla was dead, even if I had to do it like a coward. I couldn't stop myself, the only thing I could do was break His body apart. I couldn't stop at the head. Soon I had two hammers, busting open His chest cavity in a fit of rage, white blood spilling out everywhere. Organs broke into pieces, turning into a hellish soup inside of what was left of Parla. Taking deep breaths, sobbing now, I stopped.

    I recollected myself, and stood up, looking down at the mess I had made. Parla was strewn across His bed in hundreds of tiny bits, the blankets saturated with white blood. Delving into my curiosity, I swabbed the white blood, wondering why I wasn't absorbing it. With that, I was teleported back to a familiar place.

    A sea of blood red grass stood up to my waist, a calm wind brushing it against me. Standing across from me, The God of Blood and Wrath.

    Parla said in an oddly welcoming, proud voice, "Well, I didn't think you'd ever have the guts to pull something like this off. Ready to die, boy?"

Chapter 80

Nothing short of stunned, I stood still, trying to put up a front of courage. "Well, I'm sure You'll want to gloat and explain how this works now. Go ahead.", I said as condescendingly as I could, a very real fear burning in my stomach.

Parla chuckled a little, "Seeing as how you won't make it out of here, I suppose a little explanation won't hurt. The white blood, I'm assuming you saw it? That's My blood, My real blood. The offerings given to Me are what I use in the rare event that I need to knock someone, like yourself, down a peg. This field that surrounds you, every apparition that I've brought you into, they have been construed by blood other than Mine. A blow landed on Me? Bleed other's blood, not Mine. But, given you caught Me while I was sleeping, I didn't have much of a choice."

Not seeing how this information gave me any leverage, I told Parla, "You realize I'm still going to try and kill You, right?" To which Parla nodded and replied with a sense of sarcasm, "Yes, yes, I suppose that you are. And you know that there will be no holding back on My end this time, no babying per usual. I will be killing you today."

With nothing left to say, I readied a claymore, holding it out in front of me. Parla called upon His own weapon, a halberd as tall as me, held at half-mast, outstretched to point at me. "It really is a shame, boy. You could've seen more of this world than anyone else ever has. Too bad it all goes to waste here.", Parla belittled. Not as ready as I wished I was, I coaxed, "I can't wait for my own throne to replace Yours."

CHAPTER 81

Sprinting through the never ending, tall, crimson grass, my claymore was held at my side in a low guard, hoping the approaching Parla would make the mistake of attacking first. Instead, realizing He wouldn't attack first, I swung the claymore low, right across His waistline. Using the halberd's long shaft, Parla blocked the attack vertically, then cut down with the ax portion. Calling upon another sword, taking my hand off of the other, I stuck the blade under the halberd's frontal hook. Twisting it brought the halberd sideways, allowing me to get a thrust in.

Surely enough, my tip came out the other side of Parla. As though He wasn't even hurt, Parla used His pommel, rotating the halberd, to bash the side of my head. Unlike Him, I felt this, taken aback and slightly dazed.

Wasting no time, Parla lifted His halberd and tried to smash the business end onto my skull again. My sword was too hefty to maneuver fast enough, and He'd expect the sword parry again. Instead, I threw myself forward onto Parla, that way only the shaft would hit my back and the ax head would end up well past me. While this worked, Parla stomped on my foot with His own, shoving me backwards with a tentacle that came out of His chest. With my balance lost, my back hit the ground.

Looking up, I watched as the spike atop the halberd came down into my stomach, running right through me. I screamed in pain, but slowed my breathing down.

Extending a blade from my palm, I shoved a spike through both of Parla's legs, forming a latch on the backs of his heels to trap Him, and pulled as hard as possible. The God fell. Groaning as I pulled the halberd out of me, it sank and disappeared into the grass once I dropped it. Both standing now, Parla questionably didn't call upon a weapon. A knuckle connected square on my nose before I could do anything, a crunch following.

My eyes watered. With misty vision, I grabbed the next oncoming fist. Rotating to the left of Parla, I grabbed his wrist tightly and punched on the outside of His elbow as hard as I could. Feeling it flex, I did it again. The snap of a broken bone rang out, His radius bone tearing out of the inner elbow, followed by a spray of red blood. From this wound, Parla used a tentacle to wrap all the way up my own arm. Like a lever, Parla casted me over His head and well away, His forearm ripping off with my weight and following me.

Getting back on my feet as swiftly as possible, I dropped again when I saw a massive blade being thrown my way, dissipating into the air once Parla knew it had missed. Standing against Him once again, the hole in my chest slowly started to close up. Similarly, Parla's arm grew back to normal and the disemboweling blow I dealt covered over.

Parla called out, "We'll be here for a while then, no?" I hurled a harpoon back at him. Calling upon a washing pole katana, He split the projectile in half. "As long as it takes me to kill You.", I answered.

With his signature snobby chuckle, Parla replied, "You don't have that much time on your hands for that to be true." Wanting some familiarity, I encased my hands in crescent ax heads. Being resourceful with the weapon's length, Parla held the tip as far out as He could, walking this time. Matching the pace, I stepped forward slowly, my hands up, ready to box.

In a change-up, once Parla's sword tip was within reach, I used my right hand to make a glob of blood. Swiping it at the sword, I captured it, much like as if it was stuck in thick mud and couldn't move. Then, I pulled Parla towards me. Too smart for this, Parla just let go on the washing pole and let it disintegrate, bringing out a new one to skewer me with. Swinging again, I grabbed the blade once more. Attacking from every angle as fast as possible and repeating this process multiple times, Parla tried to find a fault in my guard. Inching forward with each deflection, I eventually swiped at Parla's throat, cutting through it with all four claw fingers.

Backing up and out, blood slowly dribbled down His toga for a few moments. Not wasting this opportunity, I shot tentacles out of my back and into Parla's throat gouges. Creating two sets of elongated claws for my hands, I also embedded those into His chest cavity. All at once, I cut between Parla's ribs and through multiple organs, also gruffly tearing His head from His shoulders.

Parla's head dropped beside Him as He fell to His knees, then to the ground. He bled only red, which could only mean one thing. Knowing what to expect, I shoved multiple spikes with thick ends, so He couldn't slide off of them, through Him and into the ground. Surely enough, Parla regenerated and laid pinned down to the grassy floor. I backed away a few feet, giving myself some space to react in case He tried to pull anything funny.

Parla, losing His snide tone for the first time in a long time, informed, "You've come a long way, brat. Alas, you will never be good enough." Absorbing my blood restraints for himself, Parla got up once more. "You don't have the decades of blood in your system that I do. It won't matter how many times you cut Me down, so long as I give you a papercut to tease out a drop of blood from each time, you'll never fell Me."

Chapter 82

Supposing that this was true, I needed a new plan. I couldn't kill Parla traditionally, nor could I bleed Him out over time. With no ideas in mind, all I could do was think and keep fighting. I shot a pike out of my palm into Parla's chest, which He didn't even attempt to dodge. It stuck through Him and into the ground, but He simply walked forward, letting it slide all the way through Him. I did this again, and two more times, with the same result.

Once close enough, Parla two-handed a greatsword that was nearly twice His own height, and as wide as a bartop. It dragged behind Him, the weight seemingly matching the size. Not sure what I could possibly use to defend myself against these blows, I took out two massive wall shields.

I couldn't prepare and brace now, or Parla would swap His weaponry out and catch me off guard. I marched forward, loosely holding the shields in front of me. Parla ran, using that momentum to swing the gigantic sword from side to side. I positioned both of my shields against the swing, the blow sweeping me right off of my feet and onto my back.

Parla turned his arms into rapiers, attempting to gouge my eyes out as I laid. Using tentacles, I grabbed His upper arms and held them up, giving myself a rapier of my own, to which I thrusted into His stomach. With no reaction from the opposition, I widened the blade inside of Him, then lifted Parla up by His armpits with my tentacles.

Knowing Parla would attempt to cut through these binds, I made them as thick as I could. I bullied, "C'mon, we both know I shouldn't be kicking Your ass like this. You're the God of Wrath, aren't you? What is this?" Parla didn't even fight back against me while I carved apart His chest with a pike, jabbing in and out. He snickered a little, then toyed, "I'm using the blood of peasants and priests. What do you think was going to happen, boy?"

Still sick of being called "boy", I sent the pike through Parla's heart, rotating and swishing the tip around like I was stirring a stew. Parla closed His eyes, absorbing my tentacles and pike for His own. Scoffing, I told Him, "That really is a cheap trick You keep using, You know that?"

Seemingly sick of my insults too, Parla fixed a war maul to His arm, extending out so he could use His arm as the shaft. The spiked maul came down on my head, which I dodged to the side of. However, Parla used His own tentacles to nab my shins while I was slightly distracted, lifting me up into the air upside down. The maul crushed into my ribs, multiple of them breaking. With every horrible contact bones shattered and my wind was knocked out of me. The stagger with every blow made it hard to react. Eventually, the spikes on the maul had completely torn my chest open.

Taking one from Parla's book, I absorbed the maul into my chest, keeping His hand stuck inside of me. I then continued to siphon blood, using my own tentacles to bind Parla down. Using His free hand, Parla cut and slashed away at the binds, but I just made more using His own blood supply.

"*That was it!*", I thought, *I can't bleed Him dry, not even close, but if I can use His own blood against Him, it'll run out significantly faster than my own!*" Knowing that Parla would soon find a way out of this gimmick, I caused an explosion of blood from my chest as I let Him go, sending Him flying backwards through the grass. I had noticed the once waist-high grass now seemed to rest a little lower.

Parla prodded, "I'll commend you for lasting longer than any opponent I've ever had, boy, but keep in mind that we share every possible trick, and I've been using them for considerably longer. You cannot possibly stand a chance!"

With this, a set of daggers were tossed at my head. Dodging all but one, I let it graze my hand, took ownership, and redirected it back to Parla. Bouncing this blood knife back and forth, putting more and more momentum and force into it with every volley, I eventually let it absorb completely into me and used the energy to beam a ballista bolt from my claw arm at Parla. Parla then used his tentacles to swing it overhead to guide it back at me, but I extended my own tentacle to it, gave it needles to stick into Parla's tentacles, and then started suckling off of His supply once more. Holding His tentacles in place, I watched as the grass shrunk extremely slowly, reflecting the loss of power.

Parla tugged against me, but the tide was starting to turn in my favor. His complacency would be His downfall. I hardly deserved a victory over Parla, but I'd gladly take it after everything He's done to me and my people. Standing strong, I continued, sending out another two tentacles to ground Parla's feet. I jabbed into Them, exponentially increasing the rate of blood loss. I felt as though I was a basket packed to the brim, tearing at the seams with contents.

Parla, in a last ditch effort to escape, bit His own tongue. I watched as blood poured from His mouth, to which He then spit at me. He absorbed my ballista bolt, firing it at me via spitwad. I had to move, which let Parla use a newly brandished sword to cut Himself free. Charging me while I was unfocused, Parla shoved me to the ground. I landed harshly, without any sort of padding.

There was no soft grass to break my fall, only the ground. I was close. An oncoming sword cut my human arm off, and was then wedged through that stump, across my lungs, and into my other bicep. All of the blood I had just intaken made this feel like I was only poked by a little needle. I thrusted my claw arm forward, grabbing as much of Parla's face as I possibly could. He tried to pull away, but it was too late.

My sharp fingers poked into Him as I curled them, breaking holes into His skull. Then, yanking my arm backwards, I tore the entire front of Parla's face off, catching some of His neck with it.

Parla's tongue flopped out and rested on His chest, along with His brain starting to slump out. I felt as Parla went weak, slumping back and off of me. I absorbed His sword, pushing Him off of me.

Looking down, I watched as the blood flow stopped. Parla laid limp, defeated.

Chapter 83

Wondering why I hadn't been returned to Parla's room yet, the little nubs of grass started to change their hue. They got lighter, passing into an orange, then pink, then white. Before I could realize what was happening, Two gigantic, muscled ropes tied my feet down. They were different from normal tentacles; the pure girth and strength from them was unmatched.

I watched in terror as Parla's carcass started to twitch, His face reforming. I tried to throw knives, but they dissipated and absorbed into Him before they even got close. White tissues and blood filled Parla's face back in, reconstructing what I had torn off. Then, Parla shook His head like he had been discombobulated, and said nearly fearfully, "You've actually done it, you little fucking brat. You really managed to get past that."

Terrified, I tried to use my tentacles to grab at Parla and maybe stop Him. But, same as before, they melted in front of Him and entered through His open wrists, which I could see were white. More binds overtook me, my wrists and throat now in a tight lock. Parla walked away from me this time, saying, "Now, now I'm not so sure about you, boy."

I yelled back at Him, "Get back here You Coward! Fight me, dammit!" He was running scared like a hurt dog. While His God blood was unquestionably stronger than the human, He didn't want to take a risk. Parla was afraid of me.

I watched as Parla's walk turned into a light jog, then a full sprint. I was torn, destroyed even. *"My one chance to kill the Prick, and I fucked it all up! He's running, and there isn't a damned thing I can do about it!"*, I beat myself up mentally. Any attempt to break out of the God-blood tentacles was met with no success. I wasn't even scratching them. Parla turned into a dot in the distance. I didn't yell at Him to come back and fight, nor insult Him. It wouldn't do me any good.

Once Parla was completely out of sight, the restraints against me eased. I cut through them, spraying white blood onto, and consequently, into Me.

With a deep breath, I fell forward onto Parla's bed. Wasting no time, I jumped up, not feeling any fatigue given My newfound strength. The trapdoor hatch was open, and Parla's body was gone. Climbing up, I hurried to chase after Parla, but was met with a grizzly sight. His own priests, gored, torn to pieces all around the throne room. Their limbs lay scattered, pale as a ghost from the blood loss. In their blood, written across the floor, was the phrase,

"I'm not done with you yet, Boy."

Made in the USA
Middletown, DE
20 October 2024

62455462R00167